What's in a Name

CV

D0201460

What's in a Name

MONTEREY COUNTY FREE

SALINAS
CALIFORNIA

LIBRARIES

Ellen Wittlinger

Simon Pulse

New York   London   Toronto   Sydney   Singapore

With grateful appreciation to my agent, Ginger Knowlton,
and my editor, David Gale

If you purchased this book without a cover you should be aware that this
book is stolen property. It was reported as "unsold and destroyed"
to the publisher and neither the author nor the publisher has received
any payment for this "stripped book."

This book is a work of fiction. Any references to historical events, real people, or
real locales are used fictitiously. Other names, characters, places, and incidents are
the product of the author's imagination, and any resemblance to actual events or
locales or persons, living or dead, is entirely coincidental.

First paperback edition November 2001
Copyright © 2000 by Ellen Wittlinger

Simon Pulse
An imprint of Simon & Schuster
Children's Publishing Division
1230 Avenue of the Americas
New York, NY 10020

All rights reserved, including the right of reproduction
in whole or in part in any form.

Also available in a Simon & Schuster Books for Young Readers
hardcover edition.

Designed by Debra Sfetsios
The text for this book was set in New Caledonia.
Printed and bound in the United States of America.
4 6 8 10 9 7 5 3
The Library of Congress has cataloged the hardcover edition as follows:
Wittlinger, Ellen.
What's in a name / Ellen Wittlinger. — 1st ed.
p.   cm.
Summary: Each of ten teenagers living in Scrub Harbor, Massachusetts,
explores his or her identity at the same time that the local residents
consider changing the name of their town.
ISBN: 0-689-82551-X (hc.)
[I. Identity—Fiction. 2. Interpersonal relations—Fiction.
3. Friendship—Fiction.] I. Title.
PZ7.W78436Wh 2000 [Fic]—dc21 99-30007 CIP
ISBN: 0-689-84532-4 (Pulse pbk.)

For Kate and Morgan

and for anyone who's ever asked,

"Who am I?"

Contents

What's in a Name

Georgie

Our kitchen window was only open two inches, but before I even went outside I could tell the dogs smelled particularly rotten today. Probably because it had been raining for forty-eight hours and damp canine fur stinks like old pumpkins two weeks after Halloween. I was already late for work, but I made a cup of mint tea anyway, to take with me, so I'd have something pleasant to inhale.

I live with my mother in an apartment on Mercer Street right above The Pampered Pooch. That salmon-colored building. In order to afford such luxury Mom teaches painting at the high school (where a coterie of sophomores spatter themselves with alizarin crimson and follow her around like indentured servants). Now you think you know all about me.

This much is true: We're part of the 10 percent of people in Scrub Harbor who don't live in a house they own. We're not related to anybody else in town, which puts us in an even smaller minority, and guarantees that we'll *never* find a decent place to live. And, yes, our front lawn is a minefield of poop.

You probably think anybody who lives over a pink puppy parlor must be a traumatically scarred individual. How can she ask her friends to come home with her after school? How can she give directions to her new boyfriend? How can she stand the pity in the eyes of her classmates?

I only have one friend (if you don't count MaryLinn who's thirty-five) and Christine thinks our house is "exotic" (which I think means there's only one bathroom and more artwork than furniture). There aren't any boyfriends. And what's mostly in the eyes of my classmates is boredom. They wouldn't care if I lived in a compost bin.

My mother read the numbers on the digital clock, bless her somnolent little heart. "Eight forty-five!" she bellowed from her bedroom, her face, I would bet, barely raised off the pillow. "You better get down there."

"I'm going." MaryLinn doesn't care if I'm a few minutes late on a Saturday. She remembers being a kid. Anyway, she likes me. (Which is probably more than my mother would admit to.)

I ran down the stairs so I wouldn't get soaked, and took a deep breath before I opened the back door MaryLinn left unlocked for me. Ugh. I get used to it in ten or fifteen minutes, but that first whiff of wet doggy mixed with the lemon-perfumed soap MaryLinn uses always makes my stomach a little quivery. I stuck my nose down into the plastic mug and sniffed up some mint before heading through the bathing room on my way to the reception area.

Linda already had the shampoo on a fat little beagle I didn't recognize. She rolled her eyes at me as I passed through.

"Karen's out sick. Oughta be a hell of a day. Two of us doing forty dogs."

"I could help you if MaryLinn would let me," I said.

"You're not trained. No insurance. She could get sued."

"By who? I wouldn't sue her."

Linda snorted, like she thought I'd be the first one to haul in the attorneys the minute a schnauzer snapped. Linda's not crazy about me, but it's not personal; she told me once she just doesn't care for teenagers. I figure that's fair; I'm not too nuts about them myself.

I could tell who was in the reception room before I even opened the door—that high-pitched voice was unmistakable. Every other Saturday, rain, snow, hurricane, volcanic eruption, nuclear meltdown, it doesn't matter, Mrs.

Carstenson brings her tiny, mean, one-hundred-year-old dachshund in for a grooming. And then she stands there for twenty minutes talking MaryLinn's ear off about whatever local political situation has her riled up that week. The funny thing is her daughter Gretchen, who's in my class at the high school, is exactly the same. She's president, secretary, or treasurer of about half the clubs, and is always carrying on about somebody's rights being trampled. I'm pretty sure nobody has ever actually stepped on *hers*, though. Basically she's just a big show-off like her mother.

As usual, MaryLinn turned and winked at me when I came in, then went back to nodding her head at Mrs. Carstenson's lecture. As usual, Mrs. Carstenson paid no attention to me whatsoever. As usual, her dumb dog started barking at me like I'd just broken into his mansion.

"I don't know why people are getting so *emotional* about it," Mrs. Carstenson was shrieking. "It's not as though we want to change the town's name to Camelot or something. The harbor is *already* called Folly Bay. That name is just as historical, if that's what's bothering them, as Scrub Harbor, but with so much more *appeal*. They called it Scrub Harbor after some bushy little trees that were cut down *years* ago. You see what I mean, don't you, MaryLinn?"

MaryLinn never broke her smile. "Oh, sure I

do, Mrs. C. But you know, some people were born and raised here and they just don't like the idea—"

"Oh!" Mrs. Carstenson shuddered. "If I hear that once more! Everybody was born and raised *somewhere*, MaryLinn! Just because you happen to arrive on earth in a certain location doesn't mean that it should never change from that moment on!"

"Well, no, that's not what I—"

"People need to be more broad-minded about this."

MaryLinn continued to smile, though I had the feeling it was costing her a little more right then. "Changing the name of your town is kind of a big thing, Mrs. C. People are used to living in Scrub Harbor; they don't want to wake up tomorrow living in a new place. Just because Folly Bay sounds better in a real estate ad than Scrub Harbor may not matter that much to some people."

Before Mrs. C. could launch another attack, MaryLinn turned to me. "Georgie, would you take Pattypan in and have Linda set her up for me? We don't want to get backed up. Then come out and watch the desk so I can start washin' doggies."

I took the leash of the growling peanut and pulled him through the door into the bathing room. Pattypan Squash, she calls him. I've heard my share of stupid pet names working here, but that about tops the list.

"MaryLinn says to get Pattypan set up and she'll be here in a minute."

Linda rolled her eyes again. Every time she does that I can hear my grandmother saying they're going to stay that way. By the time I got back to the reception desk Mrs. Carstenson was just going out the door.

"Sorry I was late," I said. "I guess it's a busy day."

MaryLinn was buttoning up her blue plastic smock over her wide waistline, getting ready to get wet. "Yup. Karen's out and the schedule is filled up. But we'll manage, hon. We always do." She was still smiling—that smile is practically a permanent fixture on her face, but it isn't a phony thing. I think she just feels good about her life most of the time.

She told me once she wasn't at all sorry she never got married. She likes living with her sister; they hardly ever argue the way most of MaryLinn's married friends do with their husbands. They each have their own money and they don't tell each other what to spend it on. Her only slight regret, she said, was she would have liked to have had a child. Just one. Probably a girl. That's why she's enjoyed watching me grow up. All the joy, she said, none of the aggravation.

"I guess Mrs. Carstenson thinks we should change the name of the town to Folly Bay," I said.

"Lot of the newer people like the idea. I don't know. Why go to all the bother, is the way I feel. Everybody'll just have to get new stationery. New business cards." She shook her head. "Kind of a waste."

"Those people just like to be *doing* something all the time. It makes them feel important."

MaryLinn thought that was hysterical, though I hadn't meant it to be funny. "Oh, Georgie, you are such a riot!" she said, still giggling as she went into the back room.

The next few hours were crazy. The dogs were coming in so fast I couldn't get one hooked up in the bathing room before the next two came in, and twice there were skirmishes in the reception room. The funniest one was when this little Scottie had a Labrador retriever backed up into the display rack. The big dog was already so terrified he was trembling, and then a can of flea powder fell and cracked him on the head and he lurched for the door so fast his owner practically fell to her knees.

You have to laugh at the dogs, but also, sometimes I feel sorry for them. Some of them get so scared you have to drag or carry them into the bathing room. They look at you like you're about to drink their blood or something. You want to say, don't you remember what happens here? It's not that bad. A little water, some hot air, clip the nails, and then the brush. You *like* that part, remember? But, of course, they don't remember. It's like yesterday never happened. All they know is *now*.

Most of the dogs, when it's over, are so excited to see their owners again they're practically dancing, and the owners fuss over them and say how *beautiful* they look with teeny red bows tacked to their ears or big purple bandanas tied around their necks.

But the ones that really make me feel bad are the ones who walk out afterward with their clean, lemony heads hanging low to the ground, peering up at their owners as though they're ashamed to be seen like this, as if they've been caught with their heads stuck in trash cans instead of decorated with cheap ribbon. Their tails wag just a little, like they're tied to their back legs; they toss their heads once or twice in a futile effort to dislodge their decorations. They don't feel right. They've been gussied up and they smell like a sachet instead of an animal. I know it's just soap and bows and by the next day the dogs are probably fine again, but it hurts me to see that look in their eyes, like we stole their doggy souls or something.

I had just taken Minnie, this sweet old mutt,

back to MaryLinn, and since there was a lull, I thought I ought to make up some bows or maybe dust the display rack. All of a sudden there was my mother coming in the front door, her hair bundled back in an old scrunchy, her shirt buttoned totally crooked, bedroom slippers on her feet. She looked really pissed off, and I tried to think what I'd done to get her so riled up.

She held the door open. "Come upstairs," she said.

"What? Why? I'm working!"

She hesitated for just a minute and then said, "Your father's on the phone."

"My . . . ?" I couldn't even say the word. I couldn't remember the last time either of us had used the word *father* in the last six years, which is the last time we saw him before he left for New York City to become a famous actor. I was ten at the time, and for a while I thought it was kind of neat that my dad was going to be famous. I figured I'd be seeing him on TV pretty soon. It took about six months to figure out I wouldn't be seeing him at all, on TV or any place else.

"He wants to talk to you."

"Well, I don't think I want to talk to him," I said. Although maybe I did. I wasn't sure. Why was he calling me?

"Oh, go ahead. Get it over with. Then he can feel good about himself and disappear for a few more years." My mother is not of the school that says you should lie to your kid about your ex-husband and tell her what a fine fellow he really is, all evidence to the contrary.

I yelled in and told MaryLinn there was kind of an emergency, but I'd be back down as soon as I could. She came running out holding her soapy hands up like a surgeon, scared something terrible had happened, but Mom said, "No big deal. Her father's on the phone. He thinks she's still ten. He wants to impress her with his new job."

I followed Mom upstairs and looked at the phone receiver lying there waiting for me.

"What kind of job?" I asked Mom.

"Don't ask me. Talk to him." She walked into the living room, sat on the couch, and picked up a magazine she'd probably already read.

"Hello?" I had halfway decided this was all a joke of some kind anyway.

"Georgie? Hi! It's Dad. How are you?"

"Dad," I said. It sounded like him. Like I remembered. I wished I had a picture of him, though, because I was having a hard time remembering exactly what he looked like.

"Yeah, it's me. Surprise! So, how are you?"

"Okay. I'm . . . sixteen." I don't know why I said that. Maybe because Mom said he thought I was still ten.

"You are? You're sixteen already? Jesus. Can you drive?"

"Yeah, but I don't have my license yet." I'd been arguing with Mom for weeks to take me to get it, but she was in no hurry. I wasn't going to complain about it to *him*, though. What did he care?

"I know you must think I'm a terrible jerk for not keeping in touch better than I have." He waited a minute, like he thought I was going to dispute his jerkiness. "The thing is, I'm back and forth between the coasts all the time, picking up one job or another. You know how it is for an actor."

"Sure." Those actors. No time for phone calls.

"Anyway, I finally caught a break in this business. I got a TV pilot, and they're really hot on it. NBC is ready to bankroll it. As we speak."

"Uh-huh."

"So, I'll be moving to L.A. Permanently. I think. I've got a place already and it's really big. Eduardo Silver used to live there, from that show *Guys You Love to Hate*." I was mute. "Anyway, I mean, this is a recurring role I've got. I'm not the star or anything, but I'm on almost every week and that could turn into something big, you know? So the pay is not shabby. Not shabby at all."

"What's the name of the show?" I couldn't think what I was supposed to say. This was my father, but I hardly knew the guy anymore.

"It's called *Pretty One,* and it stars Camilla Danse. You know who she is? Last year she was in a show called *My Mother, the Monkey,* but that was a bomb. *This* one will fly."

"I don't watch a lot of television," I said. Not entirely true, but I certainly didn't watch those tired sitcoms with names like *Guys You Love to Hate* and *My Mother, the Monkey.* I could hear my mother, the hyena, laughing in the living room. She was thrilled to hear me being nasty to Dad, which made me want to be nicer to him than I felt like being.

"Well, I just thought you might be kind of excited to hear your old man's gonna be on the tube pretty soon. Midseason replacement."

"Yeah," I said, trying to sound upbeat. "I'll tell all my friends." That'll take me thirty seconds.

"So," he said, and then stopped, like he'd gotten sidetracked.

"Yeah?"

"Um, I was just thinking. This is out of left field, I guess . . . but you could, if you wanted to, you could live out here with me for a while. You know, move to L.A. I mean, now that I'm thinking about it, I remember that one of the assistant directors on the show lives near me in the Canyon and he was saying that the high school there is pretty good. His kid is on a debate team or something."

Debate team? Move to L.A.? Was he making this all up on the spot?

Since I wasn't talking, he kept filling up the air space. "You don't have to decide right away. I just meant it was something you might want to think about. I mean, Jesus, your mother says you're still living over that dog place. Which isn't her fault—I'm not saying that. But still. You could be living out here with the stars."

Stars? This little laugh shot out. I couldn't help it. But when my mother gave an echoing hoot (like we were both in on some funny little secret), I pushed the laughter back inside. The guy was offering me a Hollywood hideaway. Which was weird but probably a lot less aromatic than life with the Canine Corps.

So what if I hardly remembered what he looked like? Sure, it all seemed pretty strange, but wasn't I always saying I was sick of Scrub Harbor? Sick of having no money and a mother who managed to squelch her PMS mentality for everybody but me. Here was a chance to escape, even if it did mean living with a bunch of third-rate actors.

"I hardly know you anymore, Georgie," old Dad was saying. "It might be fun to get reacquainted. We could go places together. Disneyland and Sea World. Or, I guess sixteen is a little old for that. But . . . I could buy you a car!"

"Really? A car?" Now he had my attention. My mother's, too. I glanced around in time to see that knowing little smile melt right into her lap.

"Sure! I'll be making some dough! This place I'm renting has a swimming pool, too, by the way. And a Jacuzzi. Everybody in L.A. has a Jacuzzi."

"Great," I said. "I love Jacuzzis." Like I'd ever been in one. "So, you want me to just move out there?"

When I heard the magazine slap down on the table behind me, I knew I'd hit the jackpot with that last question. Mom would be just about postal by now.

He didn't say anything right away. "Really? You want to come?"

"Sure. Why not? Should I fly out, or what?"

"Well, this is great, kiddo, it really is. Of course, I'm not ready for you just yet. I'm still in New York this weekend, tying up a few ends. And your school year's probably just getting going there, isn't it? How about, maybe, Christmastime or something? Then you could see how you like it and, if it all works out, you could start school in January. When the weather back east is crappy anyway."

I laughed, but I sounded like I had something gluey stuck in my throat, like a big dumpling from Wu Tan's at the mall. I couldn't imagine having Christmas in Los Angeles with the weather still warm and all. Santa in a Speedo.

"You probably ought to talk to your mom about this too. I didn't get a chance to mention the idea to her. I don't know if she'll be too crazy about it."

"Mmm-hmm." I suspected we both knew just how crazy she'd be.

"But I'm really glad you want to come out here and live with me, Georgie. I've missed you all these years."

"Mmm-hmm," I repeated.

"We'll have fun," he promised.

"Okay."

"I'll call you again next weekend and we'll make some plans."

"Bye," I said.

"Bye, doll. See you soon!"

I clanked the receiver down before he could and headed for the stairs. "I have to get back to MaryLinn's. We're really busy today."

Mom didn't say anything. She was sitting with her back to me, massaging her sinuses with her fingers. Why should she care? There are half a dozen high school girls she likes more than me. I ran down the stairs back to doggyland.

• • •

Usually we stop for lunch around one o'clock. MaryLinn sends me out to get sandwiches from

Esther's Cafe about a block from here. But we got so backed up today MaryLinn didn't come out to the desk until almost two.

I was just hanging up the phone. "Cancellation! The Marlows' dog is barfing!"

"Oh, thank God! Oh, that's terrible, isn't it? I don't mean I'm glad she's sick—I'm just hungry and I need to sit down!"

The rain had finally let up so it was nice walking down to get the sandwiches. The sun was coming out and the wet yellow leaves were all shiny. I love all that fall stuff: leaf piles and wood smoke and heavy sweatshirts and Halloween decorations. People in Scrub Harbor are big on decorations; they go all out. Skeletons swinging in the breeze, pumpkin garbage bags stuffed with leaves, scarecrows sitting on front porches, fake tombstones in the yards. I like stuff that happens the same way every year so you can look forward to it.

I wondered if people in L.A. hung skeletons on their porches, or if they even *had* porches. It probably wouldn't even seem like Halloween if there weren't any leaves on the ground.

When I got back, Linda was on the phone in the other room, so MaryLinn came out to eat with me. She brought us both cups of coffee, mine with lots of milk and sugar.

"So, that was your dad who called?"

"Yeah. It was pretty weird. He asked me to come and live with him in Los Angeles. Go to school out there and everything."

"No! After all this time?"

I had to swallow a big bite of tuna sub before I could talk. "Yeah. He's got a TV pilot."

"He's got a lot of nerve, is what he's got." MaryLinn blew on her coffee. She remembers my dad from when he lived here with us.

I nodded. "I said I might go, but now I don't know."

MaryLinn's mouth fell open. "You said you'd go? You'd leave Scrub Harbor to live in California? I can't believe that!"

"He lives in the house Eduardo Silver used to live in."

"Big deal. I never heard of him," MaryLinn said. "I thought you liked it here. I thought you were a pretty happy girl."

I shrugged. "You know, not *all* the time."

"Nobody is *all* the time, Georgie."

We just chewed for a few minutes then and looked out the window.

"Your poor mother," MaryLinn said finally.

That made me laugh. "Why is she poor?"

She shook her head. "I know it's none of my business, but how come all of a sudden that father of yours calls up? Where has he been for six years? All of a sudden he decides he wants you and you go running off. I know I should keep my mouth shut, but it isn't right. I'm sorry."

MaryLinn looked like she was ready to cry. I didn't know what to say, but she got up then anyway and went back inside. And then the pooch parade started up again, and I tried not to think about how MaryLinn was more upset about the whole thing than my own mother.

It was four o'clock before Mrs. Carstenson came back for Pattypan Squash, who peed all over the floor the minute he saw her. I went for the mop bucket and by the time I got back Mrs. C. had MaryLinn cornered and was waving a piece of paper in her face.

"I'm not asking you to sign it, MaryLinn. You could just tack it up so other people could sign it. I'm asking all the merchants."

"What is it?" I asked.

"It's a petition," MaryLinn said. "About changing the town's name."

I wrung the mop through the squeezer. "I like the name Scrub Harbor," I said. "What's wrong with it?"

Mrs. Carstenson smiled like her dog does, with all its teeth showing. "I wouldn't expect a young person like yourself to understand the particulars of the situation."

That really pissed me off. I bet she'd expect her daughter Gretchen to understand the particulars of the situation. So I said, "This is what I don't get. Scrub Harbor isn't the only town on Folly Bay; Greenfield fronts on it too. What if they decided they wanted to change *their* name to Folly Bay?"

"All the more reason to do it first!" Mrs. Carstenson said.

Suddenly I just felt furious. "Well, it isn't fair!" I said, probably a little too loudly. "What gives us the right to decide we can claim something that isn't even ours! Why can't people be satisfied with things the way they are instead of always trying to change everything? I don't want to live in Folly Bay—I want to live in Scrub Harbor like I always have!" I could feel my eyes getting bulgy. God, I was about to start bawling in front of Pattypan's mother.

MaryLinn took the petition out of Mrs. Carstenson's hand. "We've had a long day here. Let me sleep on it, would ya? I'll let you know." She kind of walked Mrs. C. to the door, so she had no choice except to leave, dragging her poochie behind her.

The door closed and MaryLinn checked to make sure nobody else was on their way in. "Come here," she said, and put out her arms. I let the mop drop on the floor and started crying before I even got there.

"You don't have to do anything you don't want

to," MaryLinn said, letting me get the whole front of her shirt wet.

"I know," I told her, but I was pretty sure that wasn't really true. I'm sixteen. I don't even have a driver's license.

O'Neill

O n e   d a y. How hard could it be? Tompkins thinks he's so *deep,* coming up with these assignments. "Spend one whole day being totally honest, with yourself and everybody else," he says to me. "Then rewrite the poem."

I admit my first version of "Who Am I?" (Tompkins's title, not *my* choice) was kind of a lampoon. The first stanza went:

> *Who am I?*
> *The sophomore cries.*
> *No one can identify*
> *Me—Popeye or a butterfly?*
> *Why?*

Okay. It wasn't my best effort. It's not that I didn't think about the topic, but who's going to write that stuff down where Tompkins and anybody else can read it? So now, for one day I have to exist in a falsehood-free zone. Not even so-called harmless lies, Tompkins says. "White" lies. Which are better than what, black lies? (Black flies? Butterflies? I have very little rhythm, but I've got lots of rhyme.)

So today when my idiot brother's loud-mouthed girlfriend demands that I tell her which sweater she looks better in, "the blue-berry or the strawberry?" I'm no longer going to feel compelled to say how she looks fine in both of them. Like I'm such a friendly guy.

First of all, what am I, a fashion consultant? Why does she always ask *me* these questions. I'm not *her* little brother. Sometimes I think she just wants to catch me looking at her boobs. Well, dream on, Gretchen. You look like an egg-plant no matter what you're wearing, and today's the day I'll be delivering the gospel truth.

Quincy's bellowing from the bottom of the stairs. "O'Neill, if you're riding with me, get your ass in gear."

I look to make sure he's watching, then leap up onto the mahogany banister that curves from the second floor down into the entry hall. I slide the distance, warming up my butt and ticking off my sibling. Ever since Quincy hit 200 football-hustling pounds my mother has stripped him of his sliding privileges, fearing he'll smash her 150-year-old railing into splinters. I, however, puny as I am, have never given the woman a moment's worry. Thus far.

· The big guy chews his cheek with envy. "Let's go. Gretchen's waiting."

"As long as she's waiting, there's no problem. It's when she *stops* waiting you'll have to worry," I say, ever mindful of telling the truth.

His head bobs back. "What the hell are you jabbering about?" He throws the door open and storms through it, leaving me to lock up the house (since our mother ran off with her cronies before daybreak to get the best tennis court at the club).

I get in the backseat, leaving the front free for Her Royal Highness at whose castle we stop a few blocks later. She does, at least, glance back at me and give a little wave as she slips into her rightful place next to Quincy. Younger, shorter, thinner, smarter, and with nary a girlfriend to show for my entire adolescence, I am invisible to most of the F.O.Q. (Friends of Quincy). But Gretchen, I happen to know, thinks I'm *cute,* a word she would probably also apply to that mean-tempered hot dog of hers, which howls at the front window twenty-four hours a day.

"Like my new boots?" she asks my brother.

She bends one leg sideways so it rests on the upholstery. Quincy grunts. "They're red."

Gretchen sighs; there is so much work to be

done with this boy. "I *know* they're red. I asked if you like them."

Quincy furrows his brow like this is a trick question. "Well, yeah. I mean, I guess so. Why not?"

Old Gretch was probably hoping for a little more enthusiasm. So she turns to the younger brother. "You like 'em, O'Neill?"

I lean up over the seat to see, to give the matter my considered, my *honest* opinion. Ah, Gretchen is going for the cowgirl look: tooled leather, slippery soles, toes pointy enough to stick in a dartboard. Useful, I'm sure, for riding the range. *Get along little dachshunds.*

"Hmm. Waterproof?" I ask. "Good in snow?"

"Of course not. The leather would stain. They'd be ruined."

"In that case, an exorbitant waste of money for winter in New England. But, hey, they match your eyes in that picture of you Quincy keeps on his desk."

Gretchen makes a face and turns around. I hope she doesn't think I was being cute.

"We have to hurry, Q. My mom wants me to put up these petitions around school this morning." Gretchen pulls her long hair to the front of her neck so it doesn't get caught in the seat belt.

"You know, when you refer to Quincy as 'Q' it has a rather pretentious ring to it," I inform

Gretchen, "that being the nickname of Quincy Jones and all, and since my paleface brother flunked clapping in kindergarten these two Quincys really have very little in common."

They ignore me. "What petitions?" Quincy asks.

"You know. To change Scrub Harbor to Folly Bay. I told you."

"I might also remind you," I continue, "that *we* are not really interested in hurrying to school. *You* might want to, Gretchen, and your slave here might obey your command, but I personally am in no hurry whatsoever. As a matter of fact, I would just as soon we slowed down!"

"Put a sock in it, wouldja?" Quincy yells as he sideswipes a couple of freshmen turning into the parking lot.

Gretchen turns in her seat. "What's the matter with you today, O'Neill?"

I think carefully about her question. "Well, Gretchen, since you asked, I suppose the matter with me is that I have four barely tolerable classes ahead of me today, and only one in which I normally take any pleasure at all. But despite this I get grades high enough to annoy most of the other so-called students in my classes. Which is perhaps why I have no friends."

Gretchen stares at me.

Quincy barks. "The reason you have no

friends is you talk like a frigging moron. Get a life, why don'tcha?"

"If by that remark you mean I should get a life like yours, I'd have to say no thank you, *Q*. I'd prefer to get one that had some meaning."

Quincy pulls into a space and screeches to a stop. "Get outa here, O'Neill. You're making me nuts faster than usual today."

Happy to oblige.

• • •

Great day so far. I've been smacked in the face by Melanie Anderson (for telling her her haircut made her look like Alfalfa in *The Little Rascals*) and sent to the office by Mrs. Firestone (for explaining that I'd fallen asleep because her voice has the tonal quality of a metronome). Now we'll see how Tompkins likes hearing the naked truth.

English is actually the only class I like much. Tompkins picks good books to discuss and he's big on creative writing, which can be fun. But sometimes he's a dorky show-off, strutting around the front of the room like he's on stage at the Globe Theatre. He reads passages from books in this exaggerated way to make sure we dummies get it. Mr. Melodramatic directs the school musical every fall too, so he's constantly bursting into song, which just *endears* him to the females in the audience.

We're doing a unit on poetry at the moment, which would send 95 percent of a normal class into convulsions, but somehow Tompkins makes you kind of appreciate it. For today we were supposed to read this poem "Lapis Lazuli" by W. B. Yeats, which I can guarantee you nobody but me and maybe Dana Wang read to the end. It seems kind of complicated at first, but all it's really saying is that the beauty of art lifts you above the problems and tragedies of life. (Artists are always saying crap like that; I have my doubts.)

Anyway, I suspected how it would play in class. That all anybody would really pick up on in the poem is that Yeats uses the word *gay* over and over. Poets are gay, actors are gay, musicians are gay, etc. He means happy, or even more than happy. *Transformed* by their art. But, of course, as Tompkins gives his theatrical presentation, swinging back and forth across the front of the room, book held high, the class sputters and titters and giggles, and by the end of the poem they've actually broken down into hee-haw laughter. Even I had hoped things might have changed more than that since the sixth grade.

Tompkins, however, is not bothered. He knows he's beloved, gay or not. Oh yes, he's gay. Very out. Advises the Gay/Straight Alliance. The school's cool about it—he's their poster boy for liberal chic.

Now he's inviting a discussion about the way the uses of words change over time. Do we think Yeats used the word *gay* the way we use it? Which segues into why do they think the word *gay* came to mean homosexual? Now they're all awake. The hell with Yeats, let's talk about something that has the word *sex* in it. I mean, it's great Tompkins has burst out of the closet and everything, but do we have to *focus* on it all the time? Does it have to be this groovy, amusing subject?

I let everybody else leave after class and I go up to the guy.

"O'Neill!" he says, like he's thrilled to see me. "What's up?"

"I'm a little pissed off actually," I say, smiling.

He's mildly shocked, but he pretends not to be. "At me?"

"About the poem. I mean, we read this supposedly great poem and then all we talk about is the meaning of the word *gay*."

He nods. "Well, I wouldn't say that was *all* we talked about, but I did let the class run with the topic."

"Really."

"I did it because of the laughter."

"Why did you have to cater to them? Couldn't you have just stopped them?"

Tompkins looked down at his desk, drummed

his fingers. "O'Neill, some of the kids are still uncomfortable with my homosexuality. It's early in the year; they don't know me yet. And since the subject came up this way, I thought I'd give them a chance to deal with it a little bit. To show them I have a sense of humor. That we can talk about these things."

"But they were *laughing* at you."

"I didn't feel they were. They were laughing at their own discomfort."

I consider that. Maybe.

"Don't worry, O'Neill," he continues, "nobody laughs at homosexuality in my class. Only *with* homosexuality."

What a wit. I head for the door. "I'm not worried. I just thought you screwed up the discussion on that poem."

Tompkins smiles. "This must be Honesty Day."

I nod from the doorway. "So far it's been highly entertaining."

"I'm sure you're aggravating as many people as possible," Tompkins says. "Don't forget to turn the radar on yourself, too. Less fun, more profitable."

I love how this guy hands down the tablets from the mountaintop. Like honesty is going to magically rearrange my life or something. I know what he thinks I should admit, but I don't intend to be tricked into it. I'm fifteen years old, for

God's sake. I'm not sure of *anything*. I mean, is anybody sure about this stuff?

Tompkins is grinning as I close the door behind me and walk away.

• • •

I'm sitting in the cafeteria trying to write the damn Who-Am-I? poem (which is impossible because who I am, in all honesty, is nobody). I've pushed away the inedible burger and put up my invisible shield, but obviously there are some people who don't have the common sense to leave a leper in peace. I suspect Christine Muser wears some kind of tracking device that seeks out pariahs; she's always got a slew of weirdos following her around.

But I guess she must have given them the slip this noon because she's alone when she comes up and looks over my shoulder.

"O'Neill! Are you writing?"

"No," I say, turning the pad over on the table. "I'm washing my hair." As soon as I say it I remember Honesty Day and wonder if obvious sarcasm is exempted from the rule. It hardly matters; Christine is not to be deterred. She pulls up a chair next to mine.

"I mean, are you doing homework or writing for fun?"

"Fun? Either you imagine my life to be truly pathetic, or yours is."

Christine's face crumples up a little bit, but she irons it back out right away. Okay, I know that was harsh, but this honesty stuff is making me crabby. I don't dislike Christine (I've known her since we were kids in the same grade school), but lately she seems to be hanging around me a lot, kind of insisting I be her friend or something.

You might think I can't afford to be choosy where friends are concerned. I don't know. I can see why the oddballs think I belong in their tent, but I don't want to align myself with *any* group. Maybe I just like being alone and feeling sorry for myself. (Honesty rears its nasty head again—this could get to be a bad habit.)

Christine forces herself to be nice to the jerk. "I was just going to say maybe you'd like to join the literary magazine, if you like writing. I could use a few more staff members."

I'm sure she could. I try to be a little more diplomatic this time. "Right. You're the editor or something?"

"Coeditor. With Georgie Pinkus."

Georgie Pinkus. Christine's best friend: Ms. Glum and Despondent. She always looks like she's slogging through some existential crisis, unable to make eye contact with mere teenagers.

I almost laugh. This is probably exactly what I look like too.

"What's so funny?" Christine asks.

"Nothing. Listen, I never join anything, Christine. I can't hack meetings or the democratic process or any of that crap."

She's disappointed; she closes her mouth tightly over her teeth. "Oh, well," she says, letting her eyes rest on the back of my tablet. She wishes she had X-ray eyes. Which, for some reason, makes me like her better.

"Okay," I say. "I admit it. I'm writing a poem for Tompkins's class."

Enthusiasm comes bouncing back into her eyes. "Can I see it?"

I shake my head. "Barely started it. It's killing me."

"What's it about?"

"It's supposed to answer the question, 'Who am I?' Like I have a clue."

Christine pulls back a few inches. "I would have said you'd be able to answer that question better than most of the yahoos around here."

"Are you kidding? They all have hard and fast identities: prom queen, football star, computer nerd." I gesture to my fellow lunch mates who, I notice, actually look more like pimps and bag ladies than stars and queens.

"Those aren't identities; they're stereotypes," Christine says. "You have to get down deeper than that if you're writing a poem."

"Oh yeah?" Another expert on what I have to do. I stuff the tablet into my backpack, getting ready to depart.

Christine puts a hand on my arm. "Listen, O'Neill," she says, and instantly her face flushes red. I panic. An embarrassing moment seems to be lying directly in my path and I have no idea how to step over it. I look at her hand on my arm. It's so warm it's getting my sleeve damp.

I've read books. Too many books. I know that I ought to be feeling something from that hand on my sleeve. Christine, odd though she is, is also pretty in a simple, uncluttered way. She's a nice person, and it's fairly obvious she likes me. As a matter of fact, now that I think about it—hon-estly—I know she's more than a little interested. The way she looks at me would be hard, I think, for most guys to ignore.

It's not that I don't know the truth. I've known it for a couple of years. Never more clearly than the time that eighth-grade nymphet followed me home on the shortcut through the woods and pinned me to a tree for an endless lip lock. I made the mistake of telling Quincy, who went on and on about how "lucky" I was and how I should call her up and make arrangements to run the rest of the bases. Even then, when he was saying, "What the hell's wrong with you, O'Neill?" I knew.

But what great advantage is it going to give me to fess up? To come clean with my big revelation? I'm not joining any support groups—I hate that stuff. At least now I'm invisible. Once the cat's out of the bag I'll have people whispering and looking at me funny. It's true. Even Tompkins wouldn't say it's easy. I'm fifteen. Can't I hide awhile longer?

Christine lifts her damp hand and lets the fingers dance a little on my arm. I shiver, but hate how she seems to notice and approve of it.

"I have to get going," I say.

"I was just going to say, why don't you let me read the poem when it's finished? Maybe we could use it in the magazine?"

Is that really all she wants of me? "I don't think so, Christine. I mean, I'm pretty private. I don't think I want everybody to know stuff about me."

"Well, I know," Christine says, ducking her head and smiling at my shoes. "You always were that way." Like she's been noticing me for a long time. Storing away information. Memorizing me.

I'll tell you I just felt all of a sudden broken-hearted. Like, why couldn't I fall in love with this girl? I could tell it wouldn't be that hard, if I was just different. Or rather, if I *wasn't* different. It would be easy and sweet, and she would be so happy, and I could be happy too. We'd be two weirdo lovers and we wouldn't care what anybody else thought of us.

Shit. I smiled at her shoes, and then we went in opposite directions.

Sorry, Christine. Sorry.

•   •   •

I stop by Tompkins's room after school. He's sitting at his desk reading, looking pleased with himself, as usual.

He looks up when he sees me. "Coming to turn in your poem?"

"I need more time. I started it, but now I'm starting over."

"Well, no need to worry it to death. I just didn't want you writing that lightweight crap when I know you're capable of more."

I brace myself against his desk. "I've been thinking. I want to do it right."

For a minute Tompkins almost looks worried. "Don't force yourself, O'Neill. Do what you can."

"It was your assignment," I say. "Turn your radar inward. Total honesty. I got the message."

Tompkins's lips start to move, but he doesn't seem to be able to get any words out. Finally he says, "There can be consequences. You know that."

I laugh, then knock hard on the desk, like asking to come in. "My life sucks, you know?"

"I know," Tompkins says.

"I know," I say back to him, his echo. Then I go home to write the poem.

Ricardo

Tonight I am dressing like pirate. Christine helps me with putting black circle over my eye, like so, called a patch. There is black hat and clothes from her brother who is living in college now. I think people will laugh how I look. Christine puts also many black beards on my chin. Her friend Georgie sits behind and thinks how stupid I look.

It is custom here, Christine says. For Halloween you dress so, like someone else, and everyone goes to the park to see others dressed stupid. There will be food and party. Maybe big crazy party like Carnival at home in Brazil. But not enough people in Scrub Harbor for Carnival.

Georgie don't get dressed stupid. Christine wants her wear long white dress, be American poet Emily Dickens, I think, but Georgie say don't want people looking and laughing. I neither do. But Christine likes to be my boss, so I put patch on my eye. She wears red dress and paper hair thing . . . crown. She is Queen of Hearts like in game of cards. Georgie say to her, *You don't need advertise how you love every boy you see.*

Christine is mad with that. She say, *I do not love all boys I see. You just say that because you never love any boy.*

I don't need to, Georgie say. *I just watch you get hurt. Don't need to do it myself.*

Christine shake her head. *Why you think it's only about getting hurt? Nelson didn't hurt me, did he? We're still friends.*

I'm not talking Nelson, Georgie say. *You know who I mean. The one you been crazy with for years.*

Christine look me to see if I figure out what Georgie means. But I don't know. I been living here two months only. When I come my English not good as now—I don't know what everyone saying. They talk fast and sometime I stop listening. I get very tired from hear all the time a language I don't understand. At first they want me talk to them always. Ask me, *What is like in Brazil? Like here? How different?* But I can't say right things and I get tired. Soon they don't ask so much.

Is better now. I understand much . . . many things. But not these things, who likes who. In Brazil I have many friends. Rafael like Cecilia . . .

Flavia in love with Carlos. I know all things of my friends. Here I know just a little. These are not the same way friends. No one call me up. After school they say *hi*, but nobody say, *Come my house. We watch game, drive in my car.* I wait for Christine after school to have ride home. Here. Her house. My house now too. Seven months more. Long time.

In Brazil I have girlfriend name Melissa, but we break up when I coming to U.S.A. She want go out with somebody else while I am gone. No problem. I think there be many girls in U.S.A. to date with. I don't think how hard it will be just to talk. When I tell my friends my host is girl, they say I am lucky. But Christine is too busy for dating me. And we are not the same kind. She is nice, but not for me.

Christine have many friends in school but like best Georgie. At first I don't like her. Her face is hard to me. Don't ask me nothing. But now I start to see why Christine like her. Georgie doesn't like many—Christine happy to be choosed. Make her feel special, I think.

Christine tell Georgie she have to wear *some* costume to Halloween. *Even Ricardo has costume!* she say, as if that is such a big deal. She *make* me wear stupid pirate clothes. I think nobody make Georgie do something she doesn't want.

Fine, Georgie say, but I can tell she laughing inside. I start to know such things now. *I'll be Princess Leia from* Star Wars, she say. She pull her long hair in two elastics on top of head and curl in circles. Looks funny. I laugh.

Christine say, *Even Ricardo thinks you look silly.*

So? Georgie say. *That's the point, isn't it?*

I laugh because you look like little girl now, I tell Georgie. *Not stupid. You have good hair.*

Maybe that wasn't so nice thing to say in U.S.A. Georgie look mad.

Then Christine make us go so we get to park before all the food is gone. I think maybe food will be special, like at home when we have a big party and there is lots of steak on long sticks, plenty for every. But in United States people eat not so much steak. Too much chicken. And at this big party we hurry for food, there is only American hot dogs, which I have too much all the time now. Everything else is sweet—much candy.

One good thing is apples. Very good. A game is where apples float in the water and people stick faces in water to bite one. Very cold, but I get one right away. Tastes good after so much sweet.

Christine gets apple too, but Georgie can't bite one and gets right away so mad. I know how

she feel because I have this same feeling sometime. Can't say what I want, can't make people
know me. It comes fast—I feel like I fly apart.
Never feel this way in Brazil. Everybody know
who Ricardo is at home. Here nobody know me
and *I* even don't know me. Maybe they think I . . .
stupid. When I don't talk right I feel sometimes
stupid.

I think when I go back to Brazil I won't be the
same Ricardo who got on airplane to come to
United States. Then I was a person very sure who
I was, leaving so many friends sad at my going,
and I happy to begin a big adventure. But here I
stand outside of many things, can't be part of so
many friends I want. Still, is good, I think. When
I go back to Brazil, I will be a different person
who sees the outside and the inside.

Georgie face is so wet from trying to bite
apple, she look like crying, but she doesn't ever, I
know. I am good with this game so I go back and
bite apple to give Georgie.

I give her. *Here,* I say.

She look at me like . . . scared. *You can keep it,*
she say. *I don't like apples.*

I laugh. *I see you eat apples in cafeteria. I get
this one for you.*

You look at me at lunch? she say. I know by
now she get mad about funny things.

Sometimes, I say. *If I sit with you and Christine. I'm not making list what you eat, Georgie. Don't worry.*

She look at me long time, and her face gets pink. Finally she take apple, but doesn't eat it. Wipes it on her sweater and puts in her pocket. Which I like. Why? I don't know. She keeps my apple.

Look! Christine say. *Dressed like Little Red Riding Hood and wolf!* She point at two people in fairy-tale clothes. I don't know who.

Georgie say, *Ugh, it's Gretchen and the Bozo.*

Bozo, I think, is football player I see in school. Has many, many friends.

Christine keep looking around. *I wonder who else is here?* she say. *I can't tell with the masks.*

He'd never show up for this, Georgie say.

Who would not? I ask.

Georgie look Christine. *You don't know him. A boy name O'Neill.*

This is who you like? I ask of Christine.

She look strange. *Well, I like him,* she say. *But . . .*

But he doesn't care about her one way or the other, Georgie say. I like that saying, *One way or the other.* I remember it. Someday I can say anything I want in English. I hope this is before I leave.

Let's go to the fortune-teller, Christine say. She doesn't want talk more about this. Funny. Two months I live in her house but don't know she likes this boy, O'Neill.

The trees have small lights in them so we can see where walking. From food tables to game place to haunted house where Christine fears to go. Fortune-teller is next to haunted house, which is just cloth tent, not house. Woman with not real hair, very long and black and big ear hoops. Christine wants go first.

Fortune-teller looks into glass ball. We have this in Brazil, too. Not real fortune. Woman look hard and say to Christine, *You been disappointed in love, darling.* Georgie laughs, but Christine not. *You find a better man soon.*

Georgie say, *I hope not!* Christine not listen to her—she happy to hear this news.

What name? she asks fortune-teller.

Woman look hard again. *I see letter . . . maybe F. Maybe A. Not sure.*

A or F! Christine so happy. Ask Georgie, *Who we know with A or F name?*

Adolph? Georgie say. *Frankenstein?* She make joke, but Christine do not.

I can't think of any boy names that start with F, Christine say. *But A names. Alex . . . Allen . . . Adam. Lots of them. Do we know anybody?*

Georgie say silly names. *Archibald. Anwar. Aristotle.*

Anthony! Maybe Anthony! Christine screaming.

Georgie make a face. *You believe anything.*

They argue then. Christine wants Georgie get

her fortune, but Georgie get mad. *Why I want believe somebody in bad weg* (maybe *wig* . . . means not real hair) *tells me what will happen? I want to decide myself what happen to me, not stranger tells me.*

Christine in bad mood now too. *Why you come?* she ask Georgie. *You so grouch about everything. Worse even than usual.*

While they arguing, I decide go to haunted house tent. Lots of people taking children who screaming as soon as walk in. Nothing very scary to me. I walk through dark space, skinny, don't see what is when things touch me. People in ugly costumes jump out and make noise. I think very funny. I go through two times. But children are scared, some crying. I remember be so little and scared too first time I go to Carnival. I starting to like Halloween—grown-ups act like children. Everybody dress up, get scared, eat candy, candy, candy. Is good, I think.

When I find Christine and Georgie again, that Red Hood come up and hand out papers to us. Georgie take one look and give back. *Is this your full-time job now, Gretchen? Be your mother's flunky?*

Red Hood girl is from my environmental studies class. She doesn't talk to me. The football player waits for her outside the room ever day, which I think is all she cares.

Georgie looks her so mad, Gretchen back up.

Call off your dog, Christine, say Gretchen. That I understand. Very mean to say this to Georgie: *You are dog.*

I step up. *Hey. No need talk like so,* I tell her.

From darkness come her big Bozo. *Problem?* he say.

No problem, I tell him.

I know who you are, he say. He proud himself. *You that Spanish kid. Ric.*

He's from Brazil, Christine say.

Yeah. I know, say the Bozo.

Georgie step into his face. *They don't speak Spanish in Brazil, Quincy. Duh. You ever take geography?*

They do too, he say, look at me. *What else would they speak? German? Hindu?*

Portuguese, I say. *We speak Portuguese.*

He surprised by that. *Well, gee, nobody would know that. How I should know? Ric doesn't hold it against me, do you, Ric?*

I don't know what this means, *hold against him.*

His name is Ricardo, Georgie say. *Not Ric.*

I don't mind he calls me Ric, but I don't say to Georgie. I can see Bozo and she don't like each.

What are you? he say to Georgie. *His guardian angel?*

Georgie face gets red now, but she don't say anything. She peek to see if I am looking at her. I am.

Gretchen getting left out. *Anyway*, she say, *read the flyers. There will be a meeting at the high school soon to discuss. You should all come.*

Waste of time, Georgie say. *I have better things.* She give Gretchen a big frown and I have to laugh. Georgie make me laugh. She act so mean, but this just her top crust, like on the apple pie Christine mother makes. I can tell more good things down underneath.

After they leave, Christine say Georgie, *What is wrong you tonight? You yelling on everybody.*

Can't stand those two, Georgie say. *And this silly idea of changing Scrub Harbor name to Folly Bay makes me furious. Gretchen mother just want to sell more houses to rich peoples from city who want to live in some cute Disneyland town.*

What do you care if the town change name? Christine want to know. *You moving to California anyway!* Sounds mad, which usually Christine does not.

You moving? I say. *When you moving?*

Georgie make big sigh. *I'm not definite moving. Only maybe.*

You told me probably, Christine say.

I don't know yet. Georgie sound sad. Funny how I know more how peoples feel now even I don't always know the words they say.

I hope you don't move while I still here, I tell her. *I have not many friends in Scrub Harbor. Don't want lose one.* Georgie don't say nothing, but I see she got my apple still in her pocket.

Please, Christine say nice. *Let's ask the fortune-teller if you move away. That's all. Just one question.*

Fine, Georgie say. *You won't leave me lone until I do.* We go back to black weg/wig woman. She takes off big ear hoops and rubs ears.

Can't wear these all night, she say. *Hurt my ears.*

I decide enough time for wearing eye patch, too. No more stupid pirate. Want to see now what happens.

Just answer one question, Christine tell fortune woman. *For my friend. Will she move away? Will she live in California?*

Fortune-teller look Georgie, who acting she don't care *one way or the other,* then look into empty ball to make up answer. I don't believe in fortunes either, like Georgie don't believe. But still I hope fortune-teller say Georgie will stay here. I think that what Georgie really hope too.

California far away, say fortune-teller.

No kidding, Georgie say. Christine tells her shut up.

Woman say, *I see people here and there want you be with them.*

Christine shakes her head. *But where she will go?*

She go where she must go. If California call to her, she will go there. If not, she won't go. Fortune-teller sits up again. She finish with the question.

She sure know how to talk without saying anything, Georgie say.

You aren't going, Christine say.

Maybe I'll decide when the town decides, Georgie say. *If town votes to stay Scrub Harbor, maybe I will stay too. But if they change to Folly Bay . . . maybe I will make change too.*

If you go, I'll be desolate, Christine say. (I ask her to repeat word *desolate* so I can write down and look up later. I think is good word.)

I had enough of this pretend stuff, Georgie say. She reach up and pull the circles out of her hair so it fall on her shoulders. *I am walking home, Christine. You can stay. There's Nelson. You can hang with him.*

I walk you home, I tell Georgie.

She get that scared look again. Do she think I would hurt? Never.

I can go myself, she say. *Not far. Streets full with people tonight.*

Yes, but I like to, I say.

Go on, Christine tells us. *I will be with Nelson*

until you come back, Ricardo. You know how to get back?

I laugh. *This very small town. I don't lose myself.*

So walk with Georgie to her house, not far. She live in funny place, house on top pink building where dogs go for washing. I see this before, when come with Christine. No place like this where I live. Dogs for hunting. Live outside in shed, not in house on furniture. No need to have bath.

Georgie very quiet. I guess with Georgie this means she thinking. She don't like to tell *what* she thinking.

She walk right up on stairs that go to upstairs house. *Good-bye,* she say, not turning.

Wait, I say. *Always you run away.*

No, I don't, she say. Come back down a few steps.

You have such good smell always, I say. *Is, I think, perfume?*

She make little laugh. *My mother say I smell like dogs.*

No, no, I tell her. *Is like soap and fruit . . . lemons.*

She look my face then, so I decide ask her. Can only tell me no. *You want to go out with me sometime? Just you and me. No Christine.*

She look at me a minute, then shakes head. *I don't go on dates, Ricardo. It's such a normal thing. Sorry. I don't like to be like other people.*

She make me laugh like crazy. I say, *Why you think you so strange? Nobody more strange here than me! Can't talk right. Hardly can read. Nobody knows even what language I speak. You want be different, you go on date with me!*

I can see she almost want to smile.

Where would we even go? she say. *You have no car, and there are no movies in Scrub Harbor.*

But I was thinking of this. *Best date in Brazil is get lots of friends in car and drive far somewhere. Drink. Dance. Have big party.*

Georgie frown.

But now can't do that. Have not enough friends even for little party! I say.

I hate parties, Georgie say. *I can't dance . . .* She ready to tell me go away, don't come back.

I keep talking. *But here I am different person. Now I think best date is sit with one person who like talk with me. Some person who know geography. Know I speak Portuguese. Some person who listens when I talking, even when I say thing wrong.*

I don't know, Ricardo. I don't date, Georgie say once more.

Don't say a date then. We take a walk. Talk. Stop to drink soda. Walk more. That's all.

She open mouth, but can't figure what to say. No words come.

One way or the other, I tell her. *I want to know you more.*

I see her hand grab apple in pocket. So she will go with me. Sometimes it needs not words to know.

Christine

Sometimes I wish I didn't care about things so much. It's as if my emotions are twice the size of normal people's. I'm the Arnold Schwartzenegger of sensitivity.

If I screw up and get a bad grade on a test, or if somebody hurts my feelings, everybody knows it. My face gives everything away, which is why nobody has told me a secret since about the fifth grade. I *mean* to keep secrets—in fact there's nothing I love more than knowing something personal about somebody that nobody else knows—but if questioned, my mouth opens, my chin quivers, and my eyes leak. Even if you can't read a map, you can read my face.

And I overreact. When I was dating Nelson last year I got detention one day for laying a big wet one on him right in front of the principal's office. But it wasn't about making out; Nelson and I didn't do a whole lot of that even when we were

Christine

alone. He'd just gotten his SAT scores and they
were really good. I was happy for him—too happy,
I guess—so I zeroed in with a big smackeroo. I
still don't think that was such a terrible sin, but
Mr. Flanders has *no* sense of humor. After school
for letting my emotions take charge of my brain.

So today when I found O'Neill's poem in the
box where kids turn in work for *The Pickle* (the
literary magazine) I immediately got all shaky. I
started to read the first stanza, but I was such a
mess I needed to sit down somewhere. I went
into the girls' bathroom, but all the stalls were
taken by smokers and bulimics, so I decided to
wait until after school when I could savor reading
it slowly before the *Pickle* staff meeting.

I don't know why O'Neill affects me like this,
but he always has, since I first noticed him on the
playground in elementary school. He must have
been in the fourth grade and I was in the fifth. I
knew who his brother, Quincy, was—everybody
did—he was a sports hero even then in the sixth
grade. The girls I was friendly with at the time
thought Quincy was a god, but I never saw it.

Then one day my friend Mariette pointed out
this skinny kid sitting by himself on a swing,
reading a book. I remember his hair was too long
and it kept falling in his face and he kept brush-
ing it aside to see the book. Even then, when
boys were practically invisible to me, I knew

there was something different about O'Neill, something that really got to me.

"That's Quincy Sayers's brother. Can you believe it? He's, like, totally opposite," Mariette said. "Reads all the time and never talks to anybody. What a weirdo."

We were speaking loud enough that O'Neill could have heard us, but I'm sure he wasn't paying attention. That's how he is, still. He concentrates. He's very locked up in himself and he won't let anybody in. I stood and looked at him a long time that day sitting there on that stopped swing. I remember wishing I could get inside his head and look around. I don't know why. Maybe just because I wanted to know why somebody would close the door on the rest of us so tightly. And, okay, he also has that great hair.

The Sayerses live near us, and as I got older, I began to pass up riding to school with Mariette's mother so I could manage to leave my house just as O'Neill was walking by, usually wandering along half a block behind Quincy, looking down at the sidewalk or up into the trees but never straight ahead where another person might be. He wasn't unfriendly to me. On the other hand, he wasn't exactly friendly either. He wasn't happy or unhappy or surprised. You could have looked at O'Neill's face for days (which I would have liked to do) and you'd never get a clue to what he was thinking. Which *really* made me want to know.

He let me walk to school with him, and he answered my questions (most of which I prepared ahead of time to impress him, like, "Have you ever seen *Edward Scissorhands*?" or "Have you read *Dinky Hocker Shoots Smack*?"), but he never asked *me* anything. I began to notice though that if I said something mildly rebellious, he enjoyed it. One time I said, "I hate the way all the jocks leave their gigantic sneakers untied. Wouldn't you like to step on their laces sometimes?" I'll never forget it because he laughed, *really* laughed, and looked me right in the eyes like he was just realizing I was there.

For a few days after that he talked a little bit more, and I had the feeling I was meeting somebody entirely new, a person who hadn't spent his life in Scrub Harbor, but in some place more exciting, more alive. I guess the place O'Neill really lived was in his books and in his own head. It was a bigger place than I'd ever been before. I was so happy he was letting me peek through the crack in the door I tried to push it open all the way. Big mistake. I pushed too hard, asked too many questions, and the door slammed shut.

At first I was sort of frantic and just kept jabbering at him, but, of course, that didn't work.

Pretty soon I ran out of things to say and it was too embarrassing to walk half a mile in complete silence, so I started walking to school by myself. O'Neill didn't seem surprised by that either.

I never rode with Mariette and her friends again. I couldn't hang around with those girls anymore. O'Neill had changed me. I wanted more now than giggling on the telephone and rooting for the team. By the seventh grade I knew I'd never play field hockey or organize a Valentine's dance. I knew I was never going to get up early to apply mascara so I could peer up through thick lashes at young male athletes. I knew I'd always be aware of it the moment O'Neill Sayers entered the cafeteria or the auditorium, always alone. And I knew the first time Georgie growled at me in seventh-grade algebra that she was meant to be my friend. Like O'Neill she kept to herself, pretending to need no one. Unlike O'Neill she made an exception for me.

By our sophomore year in high school Georgie and I had taken over the editorship of *Collage,* the deadly boring literary magazine nobody even read, and renamed it *The Pickle*. It was now a semiboring, sometimes quirky, sometimes downright literate magazine, which was read by a small but interesting portion of the student body.

As soon as classes were over I headed down to

the *Pickle* staff room so I could read O'Neill's poem in silence before everybody else showed up. Nelson and Nadia tend to be late anyway. Nadia only comes because she has a thing for Nelson (which she won't admit) and because I told her she really *should*. The thing is, she's so shy she hardly does any activities and you've got to have *something* to write down on your college applications. Nadia moved to Scrub Harbor from Russia in the sixth grade and her English is pretty perfect by now, but she's self-conscious about it anyway. Even at the *Pickle* meetings she doesn't say much, just peeks over at Nelson every two minutes out of the corner of her eye. Nelson, of course, is oblivious.

Nelson and I went together for about three months last year. He was my first boyfriend, I suppose, except that we were really just friends pretending to be more to see what it felt like. We broke up because he was always worried about what people would think of an African American guy dating a white girl. It wasn't even his parents—they were cool about it. At the time I was really mad at him. My attitude was: Who cares what anybody thinks? It's nobody else's business. But Nelson's a worrier. We got over it though, and now we're friends again.

Our adviser, Mr. LaPierre, was walking out of his room as I came in. Perfect. I closed the door

and settled in with O'Neill's poem. Just taking it
out of my backpack gave me goose bumps. I read:

Who Am I?
by O'Neill Sayers

If I grow up in a big house
with a landscaped lawn and a maid
to put away my expensive clothes
and I never have to think
about people who don't:
who am I?

If I live in a small town that changes
its name so it sounds like a ritzy
suburb and my father has decided
my choices will be Harvard or Yale,
lawyer or chairman of the board:
who am I?

If I spend my summers at the pool
at the country club, but don't date the girls
who won't eat lunch so they don't get
butts, and have no friends who
swagger down the street like NBA stars:
who am I?

If I don't trust anyone
but decide all of a sudden, what

the hell, to tell my big secret anyway
about how the poolside girls don't
interest me nearly as much as the boys:
who am I?

Me. I am me. I am not my house,
my clothes, my friends, my father.
I am not the country club or the town.
I am not my sexuality
or my future. Who am I?
I am the guy who wrote this poem.

I didn't move for a long time after I read the poem. I kept thinking, *I'm reading this wrong. It's great up until the fourth stanza, but then it just doesn't make sense.* I thought, *There's something I'm not getting,* and I'd read it again. But finally I had to admit it made all the sense in the world; it explained everything.

Georgie came rushing in. "Half of our staff is headed to the *other* meeting. Gretchen's stupid *information session.* Even Nelson and Nadia were going, but I told them we'd have a short meeting so they wouldn't miss too much of the Folly Bay Boosters Club. There wasn't anything new in the box this week anyway, unless you picked something up."

I looked at her, the sheet of paper hanging loose between my fingers. "One thing," I said. "A poem."

She still hadn't really looked at me. "That won't take long. We have some art from Mr. Zeno's class, but we can wait on that, I guess. I can't believe everybody is so interested in Gretchen's . . . what's the matter?" She'd finally seen my face.

"Read it," I told her, holding it out to her.

She glanced at the name on the top. "Don't tell me your favorite fellow is a poet? I guess that completes his perfection."

"Read the poem," I demanded, and she did.

While she was reading, Nelson and Nadia came in, then Ricardo behind them. Ricardo's not on the staff, but he waits around for me to give him a ride home. That afternoon my brain was so fried, I felt like telling him, "Why don't you walk home? Maybe you'd meet somebody along the way and you wouldn't have to depend on me so much?"

Of course, I didn't. I know that isn't fair. He doesn't speak English very well and it's hard for him to make friends. It's just that sometimes I get tired of being everybody's *only* friend. Georgie always tells me I'm hers (because everybody else is too lowly for her consideration), I know I'm the only person (besides Nelson, of course) who Nadia feels very comfortable talking to, and now I've got Ricardo trailing around after me too. I've got an entire brigade of friendless friends—all but the one I really want!

"Everybody else went to Gretchen's meeting," Nelson said. "I'd like to catch a little of it too if we can finish up here quickly."

"Me too," Nadia said quietly. "Even though I like the name Scrub Harbor. It always sounds pretty to me."

Nelson grunted. "The Folly Bay folks don't think it's pretty. They think it's boring. They want something fancier. Maybe they're right."

Georgie had finished reading. "Before you run off to transform local history, you need to read this poem." She looked at me. "I certainly never expected to be blown away by O'Neill Sayers."

Nelson took the poem and Nadia crowded in as close as she comfortably could to read along. Ricardo stood behind her and read over her shoulder.

"Did you know this?" Georgie asked me.

"Look at me. Do you think I knew it?"

"Are you okay? I mean, what a shock!"

I'd been sitting there cold and numb as a statue, but suddenly this heat wave rolled over me and I came back to life as a very angry person. "Why couldn't he trust me? I've always tried to be his friend! He could have told *me*!" I banged my fist hard against the table so I could pretend the gathering tears had to do with physical pain.

"Christine! I can't read this if you're yelling," Nelson said.

Georgie sat down at the table next to me and whispered, "Why would he tell you? He probably knows you're crazy about him."

"How would he know that?" I hoped I was being surreptitious about getting a tissue out of my purse and dabbing it slyly from my temples inward.

"One look at your face," Georgie said.

I groaned. "Well then, why is he showing it to me now? Do you really think he wants us to publish it?"

Georgie shrugged. "Maybe he was just letting you know."

Nadia spoke up. "What does he mean by 'the poolside girls don't interest me'—"

"He's gay!" Nelson interrupted. "Right? O'Neill Sayers is coming out! That's what it sounds like to me!"

Georgie looked at me. "That's how we read it."

Nadia was silent, but she blushed.

"Man!" Nelson was really stunned. "It never occurred to me. I mean, sure, he's not a big athlete like Quincy, but . . ."

"But, then, neither are you," Georgie said.

Nelson ignored that. "Does he really want us to print this?"

"That's the usual reason people turn things in," Georgie said.

"He wants to tell everybody in the school?" Nadia asked quietly.

"That's what coming out means. You decide to stop hiding it, tell everybody," Georgie said. "It's a good poem. I'd vote to publish it."

I cleared my throat. "Well, I think we should make sure that *is* really what he wants. Before we take a vote, someone should talk to him."

Georgie gave me this know-it-all smile. "Hmm. I wonder who we could get to do that?"

"Chris knows him," Nelson said. "Don't you?"

"Sure," I said, intently searching through my purse for nothing. "I'll call him up." I guess I never told Nelson how I felt about O'Neill—it's not the sort of thing you share with your boyfriend.

Without a smirk Georgie said, "Thank you for taking on that chore, Christine."

I remembered talking to him in the cafeteria last week, the way his arm had flinched when I touched him. At the time I thought maybe . . . oh, what's the point of remembering that now? I'm an idiot. I was in love with somebody who not only had no interest in *me*, but who had no interest in my entire *gender*. How many stupid nights had I fallen asleep imagining O'Neill would break through his shyness (I guess it wasn't shyness!) and take my hand, or pull me close, or even . . . It was so hard to convince myself that none of those things could possibly happen now, that I might as well stop dreaming altogether.

Still, still, he *was* the same O'Neill I knew.

Even if I hadn't known the whole story, I'd always known he was not like the others—that was what I *liked* about him. He was still that skinny kid on the swing set, still the gawky sidewalk looker, still the sweet-and-sour person I'd always wanted to spend my time with.

"You know," Nelson said, "even if we don't print it, all of us know this now. We can't go back to not knowing."

"Just because you know something, does that mean you have to blab it all over the place!" I said. I guess I was a little wiggy.

Nelson coughed at me. "Excuse me! As though you're not the one who tells everything she knows. My SAT scores were public knowledge in about twenty minutes."

I guess those old wounds weren't as healed as I thought they were. "Your scores were great! I didn't think you'd mind."

"Well, I did mind. I mean, the math wasn't as high as I was hoping for."

"710 wasn't high enough for you?"

"For God's sake, you two, could we *not* rehash your old arguments right now?" Georgie gave us both disgusted looks. "I think we should make a rule: Nothing that anybody turns in to the magazine should be discussed outside the staff room. We don't even know for sure that O'Neill is writing about himself. Maybe he just made it up."

"He didn't make it up," I said. "It was an assignment and it was supposed to be about himself."

"It doesn't matter. Georgie is right," Nelson said, checking his underwater watch for the fourth time. "We don't mention this unless O'Neill tells Christine he wants it made public knowledge."

"I won't say anything," Nadia promised.

Georgie gave me a funny twinkly look. "Maybe he sent it here because he *knows* Christine can't keep a secret."

"That's not true! I would keep *this* secret," I said.

"I'm teasing," Georgie said with a little laugh. Which was totally weird. Georgie is never cheerful enough to bother teasing anybody.

Georgie handed me the poem and I slipped the treasure into the front of my binder as if it were any old piece of paper. "It's actually quite a poem," she said. "I didn't know O'Neill had it in him."

"I like it too," Nadia said.

"Yeah, who knew?" Nelson said.

I guess we'd all kind of forgotten about Ricardo, or just decided he wouldn't understand the poem anyway. We were surprised when he spoke. "I think is good poem. Means: I'm not better other people, but I'm not worse. Is right?"

Georgie was positively beaming at him. *Strange.* "That's it exactly!" she said.

Personally I wasn't so sure he'd understood all the implications, but it didn't matter. I felt exhausted, like I'd been holding something heavy up in the air for a long time and it had just suddenly drifted away.

"I'm going to go catch the end of Gretchen's meeting," Nelson said.

"Me too," Nadia said (of course).

Georgie stood up, blocking their way. "Nadia, you're going too? I thought you just said you liked the name Scrub Harbor?"

Nadia glanced up at Nelson. Poor kid. Sometimes Georgie just didn't seem to really *get* the whole boy/girl thing. "I *do* like Scrub Harbor. But I still want to hear what Gretchen has to say."

Nelson left and Nadia scurried out after him.

"Nadia is right," I said. "If we're going to be the opposition we ought to know what's going on at that meeting, but I just don't have the energy. You want a ride?" I asked Georgie. Ricardo always wanted a ride. Which was too bad because I really would have liked a chance to talk to Georgie alone for a few minutes. So she could help me make sense of all this.

"Well, actually, I'm not going right home," Georgie said. She glanced at Ricardo. "We thought, I mean, Ricardo wanted to, and I said I'd go . . ." She stopped talking and got this goofy grin on her face.

"What?" I looked at Ricardo.

He seemed more able to speak in full sentences than his new pal. "Georgie go with me for walk and talk. Have soda." He looked at her and got this big smile on his face, a smile that made him seem suddenly alive, a smile I'd never seen in the two months he'd been here. "No date. Not dating. Just walking, talking. Then I take her back to pink dog house and she run up the stair."

I would tell you that Georgie giggled, except I know that Georgie doesn't giggle. Ever. So it must be that because I was so surprised and astounded and maybe even a little bit hurt by all the things I was finding out that afternoon, I heard a giggle where there wasn't one. Because Georgie wasn't interested in boys, and she certainly wasn't interested in Ricardo. Was she?

The way they were looking at each other, almost flirtatiously, must have touched off a little brush fire in my brain. All of a sudden my smoke alarm went off.

"Great, Georgie! Just run off! We should be going to that meeting as spies! The whole school is going crazy and all you can think of is going out for a soda!"

Georgie backed up. "Whoa! You just said you were too tired to go to the meeting. What are you talking about?"

I stamped my foot. "What am I supposed to do? Just call O'Neill up and say, 'So, are you really gay or not?' Why do *I* have to call him? Why is this *my* responsibility?"

"Christine, what are you upset about, the meeting or O'Neill? I thought you'd *want* to call the guy. I'll call him if you want me to. I'll just ask if he's submitting the poem for publication or not."

"And just ignore the importance of the whole thing? You can't—"

Georgie grabbed me by the shoulders. "Hey, you're freaking out about this. Do you want me and Ricardo to come back to the house with you?"

"You can come with Georgie and me," Ricardo offered. "We walk on beach where water is calm. Helps you feel better."

"No!" I turned away from them. *Me and Ricardo. Georgie and me.* What was going on all of a sudden? I may have been confused about what I wanted just then, but I was sure that watching Georgie and Ricardo gaze into each other's eyes was not it. I looked at Ricardo and thought how nice he really was and how little attention I'd paid to this person who lived in my own house.

"I just . . . I just don't know what's going on anymore!" I said.

"Listen, Christine. If you don't want to come

with us, why don't you go home and call O'Neill. You know you want to. Get it straight with him," Georgie said.

"Straight?" I said, trying my best to sound bitter.

Ricardo put his arm around my shoulder and gave a little squeeze, but as he went out the door with Georgie, he bent down low to tell her something I couldn't hear. Another secret. I never realized before just how full of secrets the world is. Everybody has them. And I guess, eventually, everybody has to tell them to somebody else.

I listened to Gretchen across the hall lecturing her audience on the importance of image in real estate sales while I waited for Georgie and Ricardo to vanish around the corner of the building.

Mr. LaPierre came walking down the hall. "Meeting over already? Didn't we get any new poems this week?"

"Not this week," I lied. It was the only secret I'd ever had of O'Neill's and I wasn't ready to share it with a teacher.

"Better luck next Monday," he said as he went into his room and shut the door.

But better luck wasn't really what I had in mind as I walked to my car and drove home alone.

If I said I didn't slow down as I drove past O'Neill's house, I'd be lying. There was a light on in his room. I know his phone number by heart.

But if I call, I don't really want to talk about his coming out or publishing the poem or any of that stuff. All I want to tell him is: I am the person I am because you are the person you are. I'd like him to know that.

Nadia

I wouldn't have volunteered to spend Saturday morning handing out flyers if I'd known I would have to stand in the rain in the parking lot of Bestways Market and that, even worse, Nelson had plans to leave halfway through our shift. I imagined the two of us standing in the sun, maybe down by the football field, Nelson talking to everyone and me handing out the sheets. Then at noon we'd quit and Nelson would say why don't we go over to Esther's Cafe and get some lunch and I would agree as I always do. And then when we were sitting there alone, I would talk to him, really talk this time, instead of just nodding and squeaking like the little mouse I am, or the little mouse he thinks I am.

A drowned cat is what I look like now. We're standing in the parking lot because the Bestways manager said we couldn't stand under the overhang where they keep the carts. "I don't want

you diverting my Saturday morning traffic flow,"
was what he said. If Georgie were here, or even
Christine, she probably would have argued with
the man, but Nelson and I aren't confrontational
like that. We do what we're told.

We've got the flyers in a trash bag, so they're
dry, and I brought an umbrella, but it's not a very
big one and two of the spokes are broken on it.
It's one my mother picked up at a yard sale, her
favorite place to shop ever since we've lived in
this country. She thinks yard sales are the best
thing about the United States, maybe the only
good thing.

Sometimes I think my parents don't *want* to
like it in this country. They complain constantly
about how much things cost, and how hard the
language is, and how they can't get decent jobs.
Who'd want to hire people who complain so
much? Besides, no one *made* them come here. If
Russia was so much better, why did they leave?

It's so embarrassing when Nelson or Christine
comes to my house (I don't invite them very
often) because my mother doesn't even try to
speak English to them, just chatters away to me
in Russian as if they weren't even there. She can
speak some English, but she thinks she sounds
silly, so instead she pretends that anyone else
who speaks it is invisible! My father will talk to

them, but that's even worse. He runs his hands through his hair and gets so excited he is almost shouting about how nothing in America works the way he thinks it should. Christine always agrees with him that things are terrible here, which eggs him on and makes him worse. Nelson, at least, just smiles and waits for him to be quiet so we can get out of there.

Anyway, I offered Nelson a chance to stand under the umbrella with me, but I suppose it was a halfhearted offer because I was nervous about standing that close to him for such a long time. He had a hood on his coat so he put it up and tied the strings under his chin. "Don't worry," he said. "I'm only here until ten o'clock anyway." First I'd heard of *that*.

"I'm here alone?" I said, wishing I didn't sound so pathetic.

"No. Gretchen said she'll drive another volunteer out to take my place. Some new kid. I don't know him."

"Oh, good." Perfect. A boy I didn't know. Even a girl I didn't like was better than a boy I didn't know. Two hours in the rain with a strange male. My stomach was twirling already.

I guess Nelson could tell I wasn't thrilled. "The thing is, I told Shaquanda Nichols I'd meet her at the BPL today. I tutor her on Saturdays now. But it's hard for her to get out here on the weekends when there's no school bus, so we're meeting in the middle."

"Mmm. The B-P-L?" There is so much I still don't know even after seven years in this country. I blame my parents for this too—they don't try hard enough to become *real* Americans and find things out. I suppose they don't know how. They ask me: *Why does this occur? How does this work? What does this mean?* I try to know everything. Maybe I don't talk much because I'm too busy listening. And still things like this happen: Nelson says "BPL" as if everyone knows what that is, but I have to ask. When will I know enough?

"The Boston Public Library. You know, in Copley Square."

I nodded as though I knew it well—the initials had merely slipped my mind. Never would I admit that I've only been in downtown Boston twice (on school field trips—it's only half an hour from Scrub Harbor on the train) and my parents have never been closer to the city than the airport at which we arrived.

"I didn't know you tutored Shaquanda," I said.

He nodded. "I'm starting this week. In calculus. The USISS program pays for tutors for any student who needs one. So it's a good deal for both of us. Shaquanda aces calc and I make seven dollars an hour."

Don't worry; I know what USISS means: Urban Students In Suburban Schools. Kids who get bused out to Scrub Harbor and other suburbs with good school systems from city schools that aren't so great.

Now let me tell you why this is *really* such a good deal for Nelson: He's got a thing for Shaquanda Nichols. I suspected it before and now I'm sure of it. Nelson Coleridge doesn't need to make seven dollars an hour. His father is vice president of a big insurance company and his mother is a pediatrician. Between playing on the tennis team and coediting the school newspaper and being on the *Pickle* staff and treasurer of the senior class and president of the Political Action Club (not to mention the time it takes to apply to every Ivy League college there is), the guy has plenty to do without tutoring Shaquanda Nichols. And I *doubt* the BPL is halfway.

So we stood there, hardly speaking. (Actually Nelson was yelling, "Folly Bay information meeting!" while I handed out soggy papers.) Why did I volunteer for this torture? At least if somebody was paying me seven dollars an hour I'd have a decent excuse for being here. I didn't even *want* the town's name to change.

Of course the organizers were too smart to admit that the meeting was really to talk everybody into voting for the new name. They pretended they were just giving you the information about it. But one look at the headline on the flyers and you knew where the organizers stood on the question. Their slogan was: IT'S NOT JUST A NAME—IT'S AN IDENTITY!

Well, that was true. Already the kids at school were calling one another "Scrubs" and "Follys." I guess it shouldn't have surprised me that most of the Scrubs were kids from my end of town, like Georgie, who probably would have been opposed to almost anything Gretchen Carstenson was in favor of. And the Follys, of course, were the rich kids whose parents had convinced them that living in a town with a snooty-sounding name was good financial planning. Christine was one of the only people I knew who lived on the expensive side of town but was still a Scrub. Of course you could always count on Christine to side with the underdogs.

"There's Gretchen!" Nelson shouted, obviously thrilled to be relieved of his duties. Right away he headed off toward her cute little car, then stopped and remembered me, looked back and waved. That's the thing about Nelson—he's so thoughtful, it's impossible to stop liking him.

From the time I met Nelson in the sixth grade, when my English was practically nonexistent, he's been nice to me. The very first day of middle school I was lost trying to find my English class and nobody stopped to help me and I was afraid to try to ask anybody, but Nelson came up and looked at my schedule and said, "Follow me. We're on the same team." And when the science teacher talked too fast and I didn't understand the homework assignment, Nelson would explain it to me after class. And when I couldn't get the history notes copied off the board in time (because I had to look up and down so much to get the spelling right) Nelson would lend me his notes overnight. It just seemed that whenever I had a problem, Nelson would be there to help. So, naturally, I became attached to him.

But now I'm afraid he still thinks of me as that lonely girl with the terrible English in the ironed white blouse and the too-long skirt, always on the verge of tears. The truth is, I don't *feel* like that girl anymore, not deep down. (My parents see the new me and they don't like her—they think she's a smart aleck and much too American.)

I am careful now to dress right. I know the places to shop to get clothes that are not too expensive, but look like everyone else's: basketball sneakers, baggy jeans, the right kind of T-shirts. But I don't know where to buy a new personality. When I go to school, even if I have the right clothes, everyone knows I am the same tongue-tied girl who feels most safe with Nelson by her side. I'm too American for my Russian parents and too Russian for my American friends.

"Thanks for standing out here with me, Nadia. See you Monday!" Nelson called.

I waved back. "Glad to help," I said. Glad to do anything you ask of me, Nelson. Just *ask*. "Have fun in Boston!"

You can imagine I was not so sincere about that. I just don't think Shaquanda is the right person for Nelson. Of course, she's black, but I never thought that mattered to him. After all, he dated Christine last year. I guess Shaquanda is pretty—for somebody who never smiles—and she walks in a very sexy way I can tell boys like. But she's so, I don't know, independent. Nelson likes doing things for people, helping out, but I don't think Shaquanda likes being helped, probably not even with calculus. She never dates anyone, although now that I think about it, she probably has a boyfriend from her neighborhood in Spaulding.

I sometimes wonder how she can be so at ease here in this school. How come she fits in, in Scrub Harbor better than I do? I've been here for seven years and I *live* in town. Shaquanda has only come here for her four years of high school. As soon as the school day is over she has to get on the bus and ride back into the city. She almost never comes to any after school meetings or sports events. Some of the USISS kids don't seem that happy here, but Shaquanda seems fine. She'd probably be comfortable anywhere. There is something she knows that I don't.

The new boy got out of the car. Nelson shook his hand, pointed to me, and climbed into the front seat with Gretchen. The boy was tall and had a long, blond ponytail, a look I don't like. It's too silly. He opened an enormous red umbrella that six people could have stood under.

"Hi, I'm Adam," he said as he approached. "And you're Nadia."

"Hello," I said in my tiniest voice. I was glad Nelson had told him my name so I didn't have to; as usual he was looking out for me.

"So, what's the deal here? We're just handing out these papers?" He reached down to rummage through the trash bag.

"Mmm. I'll hand them out," I said. "You can tell people." Maybe I could come up with an excuse to leave early; Adam could manage this job alone.

"Tell people? You mean, like, *'Read all about it! Scrub Harbor changes its name to Folly Bay!'*" He was so loud people all over the parking lot turned around to stare. If he was going to act like this, I'd leave immediately.

"Be quiet! It's just a meeting!" I said. "Nothing has changed yet!"

"I know. I'm just kidding." He simmered down and smiled. "What *should* I say?"

"Just say 'Folly Bay information meeting.' That's what Nelson was saying."

"No problem, boss. But you know what, why don't we stand up there under the roof instead of out here in the rain?"

"The manager told us not to. We'd be in the way there."

Adam snorted. "Screw that. You're already soaked and I'd just as soon not get that way. Come on." He hoisted the trash bag onto his shoulder and headed for the shopping cart area. I didn't have much choice but to follow. I felt very nervous because I knew the manager would be angry and would probably yell at us.

Adam took a bunch of flyers out of the bag and gave me half. "Here. We'll both hand them out," he said. I didn't like him telling me what to do. I'd been here two hours already and he'd just showed up, but, of course, I didn't say anything.

We handed out about three flyers before the manager came stomping out the door. His tie was blowing back over his shoulder and he was coming at us with his finger pointed. "I thought I told you kids you had to stand in the parking lot? You're blocking my customers from getting their carts."

Even though I don't like people to be angry with me, I was almost glad that Adam was getting in trouble. I stepped back, but he stepped right up to the man.

"I'm sorry, sir. My name's Adam Russell. The thing is, sir, we were getting awfully wet standing out there in the rain . . ."

"That's not my problem. You can throw those things down the sewer for all I care. Stupid idea anyway. You're in the way here!"

Adam looked around, then handed me his stack of flyers. "How about this? I can announce the meeting and help your customers at the same time!" He put his hands on my shoulders and before I knew it he'd moved me two feet to the left—then he separated one shopping cart from the pack, wheeled it around, and presented it to a woman who was just walking up.

"Here you go, ma'am. Enjoy your shopping!" He gave her a big grin and slipped a flyer in the front of the basket.

She took the cart from Adam and laughed. "Well, service with a smile—thank you very much."

The manager put his hands on his hips and shook his head. "You kids," he said. "You always got an answer." He made a growly noise in his throat and batted his hand at the air. "Go ahead. As long as you don't cause me any trouble." Then he turned around and disappeared back inside. Adam had won.

"See? No problem," he said with this big smirk on his face. What an irritating person he was. (Although I had to admit it was nice to be out of the rain.)

We handed out a few dozen more flyers without a word between us, although Adam kept blabbing to all the shoppers who needed carts. Mr. Helpful.

"You're about the quietest girl I've ever seen," Adam finally said. "Just shy or hate me already?"

At first I didn't know what to say, but the truth just popped out. "Some of both," I told him.

He laughed. "I don't believe it. Hate me, maybe, but a shy person would never have told me." He didn't seem at all bothered that somebody would decide to dislike him after only twenty minutes.

"How long have you lived here?" I asked him. I usually don't ask people questions, but I guess he made me curious. Who was this person who said whatever he pleased to people he hardly knew?

"Couple of weeks. Now, don't you feel sorry for me, having to move at the beginning of my senior year in high school?"

I thought about it a minute. "I would feel sorry for some people that happened to. But you're not the kind of person who needs anyone to feel sorry for him," I said.

Adam reeled backward, pretending I'd wounded him. "Whoa! How do you figure that, Dr. Freud?"

I was tired already of his joking around. "Because I know how it feels to be new someplace and not fit in and wish you were invisible. But you aren't like that. You like being new. You want people to notice you."

I thought he would make some remark right back to me, but he didn't. He wheeled out a few more carts and then said, "I do like people to notice me. You're right. But that doesn't mean it's easy to start a new school in your senior year."

"I suppose," I said. Really, I didn't feel like talking to him at all.

"So when were you new?" he asked.

"Seven years ago."

"Seven years? You're practically a townie by now," he said.

That made me laugh, but not in a funny way. "You think so? You don't know Scrub Harbor then. And you don't know me either."

He wasn't smiling so much anymore—that was good—his smile was not a real smile, not one to trust. "No, I don't. So tell me more. Where did you move here from?"

I sighed. I hadn't had to tell my story in so

long—my friends had known it for years—and it made me tired to remember it.

"We came from Russia," I said, wishing I wouldn't have to say more, but knowing he would ask.

"Wow! Russia! Did you escape? I mean, was it hard to get out?"

"No, not by then. My father had some relatives living here and they bragged about how good their life in America was. My father was mad he couldn't have such a great life too. He thought, why should his rotten cousin have all the luck?" Why was I telling him all this? I was talking too much.

"So now your dad's happy?"

"No. His cousin was lying."

Adam laughed loudly, then stopped himself. "Sorry. I wasn't laughing at your dad. You just tell it so funny. So, what does your dad do now?" He was staring at me as if my story was fascinating. I wasn't comfortable with his eyes resting on me so long, expecting something from me, and yet making someone laugh was such a feeling!

"In Russia he was an illustrator—an artist. Here he's a house painter. And twice a week he drives the Eldervan from the Senior Center to the shopping mall and back." I made a scale with my two hands full of papers. "So there's good and bad. He hates the house painting, but the old ladies from the center are always bringing him coffee cakes, and at least now he can fight with his cousin in person instead of through the mail."

I was a little disappointed Adam didn't think that was so funny. He passed carts to a few more shoppers while I slipped flyers into the baskets. His smile was more relaxed now, but he still had more questions. "Did you speak English when you got here?"

I shook my head. "Not much. I learned fast though. I had to."

"Well, no wonder it was so different for you. I mean, I just moved from Vermont! I could already speak New England."

He wanted me to laugh at that, but all I gave him was a weak grin. This Adam just liked himself too much. And he couldn't believe that I didn't. He didn't care about *me*—he just couldn't bear the fact that somebody on earth wasn't charmed by him.

"Nadia, is that you?"

It was hard to make out the face underneath the big yellow rain hat, but I recognized the paint-splattered jeans and Mrs. Pinkus's voice. Georgie's mother—my art teacher. "Hi, Mrs. Pinkus." I was always kind of confused about how to act around her—was she the person who encouraged me to try new painting techniques in class, or the one who made me wish I wasn't there

when she yelled at Georgie about forgetting to
unload the dishwasher or take out the trash?

"You're not involved in this Folly Bay non-
sense, are you?" Mrs. Pinkus asked. She always
comes right to the point.

"I'm just helping hand out flyers about the
meeting," I said. "I don't think I'm in favor of
changing the name."

"Well, I hope not. It's the silliest thing I've
ever heard." She took a flyer from my hand.
"Look at this! 'IT'S NOT JUST A NAME—IT'S AN
IDENTITY.' *Exactly*. Scrub Harbor sounds like a
place where people work hard and appreciate the
beauty of the spot they've settled in. Folly Bay,
on the other hand, sounds like a vacation spot for
nitwits."

Georgie would have hated me for thinking it,
but sometimes you could certainly tell that she
and her mother were related.

"Sometimes change is good for a community,"
Adam chimed in. Couldn't he ever shut up?

"Do I know you? Are you at the high school?"
Mrs. Pinkus asked.

"I'm Adam Russell. Senior. New this year."

"Mrs. Pinkus teaches art," I explained, then
waited patiently for her to shred Adam's little
homily into a hundred pieces.

"Well, Adam, I think change can be terrific
too, but change for its own sake, just because

people have nothing better to do with their time, is a waste. In this case, a waste of taxpayers' money for a special vote, and a waste of people's energy that could be far better spent. Mine included." She smiled and put the flyer back on top of my pile. "And yours, too, Nadia. Go home and paint me a picture. Of *Scrub Harbor*!" she called as the market door closed behind her.

"Wow, she's opinionated, isn't she?" Adam said.

"*She* is? You're the one who's opinionated. You've lived here for five minutes and you've got a comment to make about everything."

"Well, why shouldn't I? You've got your share of opinions too. I admit, you don't always say yours out loud, but it doesn't take a mind reader to see the judgments passing over your face like a bad weather pattern."

"What?"

"How come you don't like me? Because you're a Scrub and you think I'm a Folly? I don't care one way or the other about this stupid name business. I only went to that meeting to get to know some kids. So I'm not a complete stranger to my entire graduating class."

What a nerve this guy had! "What makes you think I'm a Scrub? Because my father is a house painter?"

"What? No! You just told that teacher . . ."

"You'll fit right in here, Adam, because that's the way this town thinks! We were Scrubs and Follys before anybody ever thought up changing the name. They ought to just split the place down the middle and then we could both have the name we deserve! The rich people could be Folly Bay and the rest of us could keep the old name, just the way we keep all the other old things in town, the old houses, the old cars, the old people."

I was getting a little off the track, but, damn that Adam, he was really making me mad. He expected to sail into town and be everybody's best friend overnight. He expected to be somebody in three weeks when I was still nobody after seven years. He expected it because of who he was; I don't care if he grew up in Vermont or California or Alaska, he was a Folly, for sure.

We missed about a dozen potential flyer receivers, and now we were even blocking people's paths to the shopping carts, but I was sick of the whole thing anyway.

"Why are you getting so mad?" Adam had one palm spread out over his heart as though he was the most sincere guy around. "I'm not even part of this town! How come I'm getting the blame here?"

"You know what? I'm really tired of discussing this. I'm wet and I'm cold and I'm going home." I handed him the trash bag with the rest of the fly-ers in it. "Have fun."

"Wait a minute," he said. I turned around just far enough to see him stick the whole bag into a big trash barrel by the door of the Bestways. "I'm not standing out here alone. I don't even give a damn about this meeting."

I kept walking, putting my broken umbrella up again, though at this point it wasn't going to make much difference. It was a twenty-minute walk home, but I'd concentrate on the bath I intended to take when I got there.

"Will you just wait a *minute*?" Adam said again as he came alongside me.

"What for? It's raining."

"No kidding. I thought maybe we could go get something to eat. Together. There's this deli place I saw just down the block."

I stared at him. What was he trying to pull now?

"Smoke the peace pipe?" He looked so sure of himself. I guess the girls in Vermont all fell over when he gave them that trust-me smile.

"Not a good idea," I said. "We wouldn't get along. I'd rather go home."

Adam shook his big red umbrella so it popped up practically in my face. "Fine, but one of these days that big attitude of yours is going to get in your way. There's such a thing as being *too* sure of yourself, you know." He turned around and stalked off down the sidewalk in front of the mall.

My mouth was hanging open so far I was taking in rainwater. My big *attitude*? Too *sure* of myself? Where was he getting that? I was a mouse! A chicken! Invisible even to my friends! No more than a minor annoyance to the person I'd worshiped for seven years!

But Adam Russell, who'd known me for less than an hour and a half, who had hair too long and a laugh too loud, who'd probably left girls weeping in Vermont, who'd invited me to make peace at Esther's Cafe—Adam Russell thought I was sure of myself. *Too* sure, as a matter of fact.

And for just a minute or two I thought, *Maybe I am*.

Nelson

We'd been poring over derivatives for more than two hours already and my neck was tired of being turned sideways, crooked, and upside down to check Shaquanda's calculations without having it seem like I was trying to crawl into her lap at the same time. Oddly, she didn't seem to need all that much help. She was a little unclear about logarithmic functions, but she understood my explanations right away. Mr. Armbruster had given me some practice sheets and Shaquanda made me do them too. I swear she was trying to finish hers before I did.

We were sitting at a long table in a room full of long tables. There were windows at one end of the room, but we were so far away from them that, after sitting so quietly for so long not talking about anything but numbers, you could actually start to believe there was no outside: no sun, no breeze, no traffic, no noise. I'd always liked that about libraries, the way you felt surrounded by the huge, warm silence. But being with Shaquanda made me restless. At the very least I needed to move and speak and look at her face.

Finally at about one o'clock, when we'd gotten through all the sheets, I called a halt. "I'm starving. Let's go get some lunch."

"I brought a sandwich," she said, not looking at me. "To save time."

"Please! Shaquanda, nobody can do calculus for more than two hours without a break! There's a great Thai place right across the street where my dad always eats."

She looked uncertain. "Thai? Like from Thailand?"

"Yeah, you know. Pad Thai? Noodles and peanuts and bean sprouts." I'm not dim. I know she lives in Spaulding and doesn't have piles of money and might not ever have eaten in a Thai restaurant before, but I didn't think I should act like I thought that.

She gave me a long look, almost a dare of some kind. "Well, I'm not a big bean sprout fan, but if you're buying . . ." She didn't finish the sentence.

"Of course I'm buying. I invited you," I said. Really, the whole thing was kind of ridiculous. I was getting paid a measly seven dollars an hour to tutor somebody who didn't even seem to need

tutoring, and now I was going to spend my earn-
ings taking her to lunch. Not that I minded. I
would have *paid* to tutor Shaquanda Nichols. I'd
been looking forward to it all week.

I'll admit that until this year I never paid
much attention to Shaquanda, even though she's
been in many of my classes the past four years.
You might think we'd have been friends right
along since she was one of the only other African
Americans taking honors classes. Since there are
only a handful of black families living in Scrub
Harbor, there aren't more than a few of us at the
high school at any one time. There was a girl a
few years ahead of me doing honors; our parents
were kind of friendly, but I never knew her that
well. And my freshman year there was another
USISS guy from Spaulding who was doing honors math and science. Lou Hillyard.

Actually I did get to know Lou a little bit. I
liked him. He was kind of a hotshot kid, always
showing off in class. Which plenty of the white
kids did too, especially freshman year when a lot
of people are in a hurry to make a big impression.
Lou came over to my house a few times—he said
he wanted to be a doctor and my mother spent
one entire afternoon telling him all about medical
school. Then he didn't come back to Scrub Harbor
sophomore year. I guess he just went to school in
Spaulding—I never heard from him again.

Anyway, it didn't seem like I had much in common with Shaquanda. We were always friendly, but never friends. Maybe because the thing with Lou didn't work out. I guess I thought, why get involved with the Spaulding kids—they aren't really like you anyway. That sounds awful, I know, but it's true. Most of them have this tough act going where they pretend they can't even see anybody else except the other kids in the program and a few white kids who hang around wearing hip-hop clothes and worshiping them. Most of them have a swagger I could never master and a lingo I can barely understand. And they don't seem that anxious to talk to me either.

But for some reason, this year Shaquanda seems different. Now that everybody's talking about where they're applying to college I'm thinking about the future. Suddenly I realize we're not all going to be spending the rest of our lives in Scrub Harbor. Especially the honors kids. Next year we'll be in schools all over the place, and it won't matter whether we grew up in Scrub Harbor or Spaulding or New York City. I'm sure Shaquanda will be going to college too, which makes her seem more *like* me than *unlike* me.

And besides, she gets better looking every year. She has the most beautiful black skin I've ever seen, and it's stretched over just the right amount of everything underneath.

It had stopped raining by the time we came out of the BPL, which made me feel a little less guilty for running out on Nadia. I was hoping she managed to speak to that Adam guy. It wouldn't hurt her to make a new friend. It wouldn't hurt me either.

Don't get me wrong. Nadia is a nice girl, but she depends on me too much. We're seniors. Next year she'll have to figure out how to make friends on her own. I do feel a little mean, like I'm pushing her out of the nest, but it's for her own good.

We got a window seat at the restaurant and the waiter brought menus. Shaquanda looked a little puzzled as she read hers over and I wondered if I should have gone with less exotic food.

"Would you like me to order for you?" I asked. I don't know what made me think of that option. Some old movie maybe.

She looked astounded at my offer, which was obviously ridiculous. "The menu is in English, Nelson. I can *read*."

"I know you can read. I just meant . . ." God only knew what I'd meant.

But then her face lit up. "They have curry! I love curry—my uncle makes the best! That's from Thailand?"

I nodded, eager to reclaim my authority. "I think it was an Indian food originally, but a number of cultures do curry dishes. Each of them does a different adaptation of it, of course. A Thai curry, for example, will be made with coconut milk whereas an Indian curry is more likely to use a meat stock."

Shaquanda tried to stifle her grin. "Really? I'll try to remember that," she said.

I blushed. I am not usually this much of an asshole. I don't think. I decided it was finally being able to sit across from Shaquanda and watch her slowly blinking eyes search the menu that had so stupidly loosened my tongue.

She ordered the Masaman curry with chicken and I ordered a yellow vegetarian curry, and even that seemed dumb. Why didn't I order it with beef, which I like better anyway? As though the person I was pretending to be wouldn't eat meat or something.

Now that I was done teaching her math, I felt off balance, like no decision I made would be right. I'm not usually such a goofus around girls—I dated Christine for months last year and another girl the year before that and they both still like me, even though we broke up. And, of course, Nadia is my shadow. I'm *used* to girls, which made it all the more confusing that I'd become a dumbbell in the time it took to cross Boylston Street.

I decided to try to put things right with a com-

pliment. "You know, you have a good under-
standing of calculus. I'm surprised you're not
doing well in Armbruster's class."

"Oh, I'm doing all right. I just want to do better," she said.

"What's your average in there?"

She pursed her lips and thought back over the
term. "I should have a B+ going."

"B+? Here I thought you were scraping by
or something. B+ in honors calculus is good!" I
tried to think back over our lesson; had I been
very condescending about my abilities in math?

"I know it's good," she said.

"Well, why did you ask for a tutor then?" A
thought crossed my mind. Somehow she'd known
I would be the tutor; this was all a ruse to spend
time with me. IIa!

"I asked for a tutor because B+ is *good*. Are
you getting a B+ in there?"

"I've got an A, I guess." Why should I feel
embarrassed about that?

"No kidding. And would you be satisfied if you
had a B+?"

Talking to her was like dodging snowballs. You
never knew where the next one was coming from,
and sooner or later you knew you were bound to
get hit.

"My father wouldn't be satisfied," I said, giving
a little laugh.

"Well, my mother isn't satisfied either. And neither am I. And neither would you be, you liar."
She didn't say it in a mean way—in fact, she said it
jokingly, but it hit me anyway, right in the face.

I guess she could tell I was a little stunned.
She waited until the waiter had put our lunch in
front of us and refilled the water glasses, then she
said, "I guess that's why I asked for you to tutor
me. I wouldn't be comfortable raggin' on a white
boy like that."

"You asked for me?" I tried to take a little
comfort from it.

"Of course I did. It's not so bad that *you* think
you're smarter than me—though you're not—but
I really can't take that attitude from white kids.
Like they're gonna reach way down and do me a
favor."

I was speechless. So much information to
take in. She chose me, but she was smarter than
me (how did she figure *that*?); she thought the
white kids looked down on her, but I didn't.
Which, if any, of that was true seemed impossible to figure out.

"I like the curry," she said, "but it isn't nearly
as hot as my uncle makes it. His is fiery." She
looked up. "I know, every culture makes it differ-
ently."

I decided to go for a slight change of topic.
"What schools are you applying to?"

She shrugged. "UMass, Boston University, maybe Suffolk."

"Really? What's your class rank?"

She sighed. "Ninth. I didn't have a great attitude my freshman year and it's kept me down a little. I could swing up to eighth by the end of the year, though. Especially if I get an A in calculus."

"That's terrific."

"Not as good as you, Number Two."

I was flattered that she knew. "And likely to remain so since Sarah Tolliver has a lock on valedictorian. So, are your SATs exemplary too?"

"They're good enough. I know what you're gonna say. I should be applying to Ivy League schools or something."

"Well, you could. Why not, if your stats are this good?"

She shook her head. "No, thanks. I have to stay around Boston. My mother has three kids at home and I help her out. Besides, why should I pay to be stuck in one of those little dorm cells with somebody I hate?"

"You could at least apply to Harvard. That's close enough to commute." Even as I said it, I thought of the application I'd mailed off last week in order to be eligible for an early decision. If it was up to my father that application would leap to the top of the pile and demand an acceptance letter.

She read my mind. "How many of us would they take from one small school? I mean, you're on track for Harvard, aren't you?"

"How do you know *that*?"

"I make it my business to know things." She subdivided the last of the curry on her plate so that each bite of chicken had a little pillow of rice around it.

"Even if I get into Harvard, that doesn't mean you wouldn't."

She shrugged. "Harvard's not for me. I walked around over there once, sat on the steps of that big library. It didn't feel right. It's not who I *am*, you know?"

I nodded, although I didn't have a clue who she thought she was, or who she thought I was, or who Harvard thought either of us might be. I called the waiter back over to order some tea.

Shaquanda got up to call her mother to let her know when she'd be home. "I guess we're done with tutoring for today?"

"I can't imagine what else I can show you."

"You just don't want me gettin' that A+ before you do," she said, and then walked slowly down the aisle to the back of the restaurant. I was not the only male in there who watched.

I liked this girl, even more than I expected to. I liked the way I never knew what she'd say next;

even when it made me feel stupid, it was thrilling. But I had the distinct feeling I'd been lumped into the same category as Harvard: We weren't for her.

By the time she got back, the tea was cooling off already. She must have called every relative in the phone book.

"Everything all right?"

"Mmm. My mother gets upset when my older brother, Darius, doesn't get home on time. Or call. I had to call around and locate him."

"Couldn't your mother have done that?"

Her lip curled to one side. "I have certain phone numbers that she doesn't. You know how it is—you don't want your mother knowin' everything."

"So how come he didn't call her?"

This time her lips parted slowly and she laughed. "You are such a good boy, aren't you, Nelson? I'll bet your mother has never lost a moment's sleep over you."

I could feel my ears heat up. "Well, why should she? What's the point of worrying people who love you?" Her more-sophisticated-than-thou attitude was starting to annoy me.

Her smile slowly collapsed inward. "No point. No point at all." She sat there wrapping the string of the tea bag tighter and tighter around the spoon, as though she were trying to cut off its circulation. I watched her for a full minute, mesmerized.

Find another topic. "Do you remember a guy named Lou Hillyard? He was in USISS our freshman year." I'd been thinking about old Lou today anyway.

She looked up sharply, as though the question had startled her. "Sure, I know Lou. I went all through elementary school with him."

"Yeah? Whatever happened to him? Why didn't he come back to Scrub Harbor?"

She picked up her cup and stared into it like she was reading tea leaves. "He hated the damn bus ride."

"The bus ride?"

She nodded. "It *is* awful. You get up at five thirty so you can leave Spaulding by six forty-five and then you sit in that crowded, drafty bus that stops in three other towns and heats up to a hundred and twenty degrees before it lets you off in Scrub Harbor. We all hate it. But Lou just couldn't *stand* it. He even hated getting off the bus, while all the Scrub Harbor kids were getting dropped off by their mothers in minivans and big old Volvo station wagons. I guess he just hated everything about it."

"Man, I never realized that."

"You knew him real well?" Her sly smile seemed to be laughing at me again.

"No, not real well, but I *knew* him. He never told me that."

"He wouldn't tell you, Nelson. You'd have to be on the bus to know it."

I let that pass. "So, he goes to Spaulding High School now?"

She shook her head and sipped her tea. "He's in jail. Last I heard."

"What? Why is he in jail?"

She sighed and looked out the window. "He didn't kill anybody. I don't know. Some drug deal, I think. I forget exactly."

"You don't remember why he's in jail?"

When she turned to face me again, anger was sparking in her eyes. "You expect me to remember the rap sheet on every juvenile delinquent in Spaulding? I know, you talked to him twice and you thought he was a real prince, but Lou Hillyard was never a guy who was gonna make it. He let everything get to him. I could have told you that back then."

I picked up my cup of tea, but instead of drinking it, I just stared down into it and let the steam warm my cheeks. "I'm not as big a jerk as you think I am," I said.

"I don't think you're a jerk." She sighed again,

a heavy sigh. "You don't know a damn thing about being black, but I don't hold that against you. You were lucky to be raised in a place you didn't have to know."

"Well, that's bullshit!" As a rule I don't like to swear, but I didn't even think about it this time. It was the only word that seemed to apply. A woman at the nearest table turned halfway around to look at me.

"Is it? All your friends are white. Don't you just forget sometimes that you aren't white too?"

"Not for a minute. And that's *why* I don't forget it. Because no matter how many A's I get or how many clubs I'm president of, I can't make there be no difference between us. They're my friends, but I'm their *black* friend." Even as I said it I knew two things: That it wasn't true for everybody (probably not Nadia or Christine), and that it was so true for most people it made me feel sick.

Shaquanda was quiet while I got my wallet out and paid the bill, leaving a hefty tip since we'd been sitting there so long and talking so loudly. I imagined Shaquanda was counting up the cash on the table and thinking, *You're such a good black boy, Nelson.*

I followed her outside. The afternoon had gotten windy and we zipped up our jackets. "What subway do you take? I'll walk you."

"You don't have to."

"I realize that. What subway do you take?" I knew I sounded angry, but I couldn't help it.

"Green line. Just down the block."

I nodded. "I get on there too. Going the other way, of course."

"I'm sorry I pissed you off back there. I say what I think, Nelson. Sometimes people don't like that—"

"Would you go out with me?" I said, interrupting her. What was there to lose now?

She stopped walking and looked at me. "Where? You mean, like a date or something?"

"What else would I mean?"

"I don't think I've ever been asked out that way before. Like, so formally."

I groaned. I would never do *anything* the right way with this girl.

"Let me ask you this," she continued. "Have you ever dated a black girl before? I know you've had white girlfriends—"

"What was my choice? I hardly knew any black girls."

"You knew me."

"Let's just say you were a little intimidating."

She liked that, I could tell. "So you liked dating white girls? They weren't so *scary*."

"I liked the girls I dated, yes. But it didn't make me feel white, if that's your next question. It made me feel . . . exposed. Different. Black."

She looked at me through half-closed eyes as though the truth could not be disguised if you saw it out of focus. I was about to tell her to just forget the whole thing when she said, "You realize I asked for you to tutor me even though I knew you didn't need the money. I knew if you agreed it would be for some other reason."

I stared at her. "What other reason would that be?"

"God, Nelson, don't be dense," she said. "I know you like me."

"You do. You know that." I felt like I was sliding down the side of a large building and there was no place to grab on.

"So, where would we go on a date?"

I couldn't imagine. Getting through another five minutes with her seemed impossible; how could we go on a date? "What most people do. I don't know. Go to a movie?"

She didn't say anything while we sprinted across the street through traffic to the subway station. I could see this guy standing there from ten feet away and I made a quick decision, the way you always do. I didn't know what Shaquanda thought you ought to do when you saw a young black guy shaking a paper cup at the subway entrance, rattling a few coins and asking for more. I couldn't even imagine. So I decided to do what I usually do, what my father does.

I reached into my pocket and brought out a handful of change, quarters, nickels, dimes, and tossed the whole batch into the cup. It made too much noise and I was immediately embarrassed, as I always am in that situation.

"Thank you, kind sir!" the man said jovially, then noticed my companion. "Hey there, girl! Wuz my Shaquanda doin' roamin' roun' wid dis rich boy?"

"Hey, Jerome. Wuz happ'nin' wichu?" I stared at her; I couldn't help it. Not that I hadn't heard the other USISS students speak like this to one another—I had, plenty of times. But never Shaquanda. She spoke the way all the honors students spoke.

"You tell Darius he better get his ass up to see me one a dese days," Jerome said.

"I will!" Shaquanda waved to him as she ran on down the stairs and around the corner. I hurried to catch up, but for some reason she seemed able to swim right through the oncoming crowd that knocked me around like a tidal wave. I rounded the corner and saw that she'd stopped at the spot where we'd have to part ways, her to go south, me north.

"He's a friend of my brother's," she said, though I hadn't asked. "He's not a bad guy. Just can't hold a job."

"Yeah. He seemed nice." What was I supposed to say? I ask you—I gave the guy some change—how was I supposed to know the ramifications of my small generosity?

She gave this really nasty laugh. "Yeah, he sure *seems* that way, doesn't he? He shakes that cup the way a *nice* person would. Listen, Nelson, I thought maybe I could go out with you. But I can see now that's just not going to work out."

My head felt like one of those microwave pop-corn bags when it gets real big and hot enough to explode. "Why not? Because I can afford to throw away some change? Because I didn't have a big conversation with your buddy Jerome? Because you're embarrassed to be seen with somebody who's not black enough? Or because I'd be a more acceptable black person if I didn't have money? Which is it? I think I should at least know my crime."

She locked her jaw and stared me right in the face. "You're not a bad guy, Nelson, but I can't go out with somebody who feels sorry for me."

"What?" I tried to protest, but she kept on talking.

"Maybe you can't help it, but you do. The way you talk to me and smile at me . . . the way you looked at Jerome . . ." She put her hand on my arm for just a second, then let go. "Tell you what. Sometime, after we both grow up and finish col-lege and start living our real lives, you call me up and we'll . . . go to the movies."

"You think I'll be blacker by then?" I felt like there was sand in my mouth, wet sand that I could neither spit out nor swallow.

"I think we'll be who we are by then," she said. A train whistle blew like a shrill wind through the station as she disappeared down the tunnel.

Shaquanda

"Yo, Shaq! I heard me a rumor yesterday."

It was one of those sophomore nitwits calling me from the back of the bus. Cornell or Leon or one of those. No need to respond—that only made them worse.

"I heard you's got a new man. I heard you's making it with Nelson Mandela, Shaq. Mr. Black America."

"Shit, he ain't black, Leon," somebody else said. "He's a zebra. Black and white stripes."

"Skunk's more like it." They howled with laughter.

"Hey, Shaq—"

"My name's not Shaq, you hear me, little boy?" I wiggled my pinkie at him so the others would laugh at him and get off my back. We were almost to Scrub Harbor where I could get out of that damn yellow oven that everybody recognized as we careened up the coast from one pretty little town to the next. Here come the USISS kids. The USELESS kids. The kids in the *program*. The poor kids, the black kids, the lucky kids (though they don't appreciate it) who we so kindly allow to attend our marvelous suburban schools. Six months more, and then I'd never ride a school bus again.

By the time we've come this far, and the kids who get off in Kettering and Wells and Aylesbury are long gone, most of us who're still on the bus have gone crazy with the heat and the boredom and the knowledge that nothing but another long day of classes is waiting for us when we finally do manage to get off. This is the time of the morning when fights are most likely to break out, when couples are most likely to break up, when Lenny, the driver, is most likely to break down and start yelling at everybody. This is the time Lou Hillyard stood up and announced to the whole bus that he'd be goddamned if he'd spend the next three years crammed into a sardine can with a bunch of suckers and losers running away from themselves. This is the time I usually try to go inside my head where it's quiet, the only place I can be alone.

But the bus crazies were out to get me. Leon had kept up his harangue from the backseat even though I was ignoring him. Jasmine, a girl who usually would not risk her ice-cold reputation to talk to anybody who actually made an effort in life, left her seat to come and share mine.

"Girl, izat true? You makin' it with Nelson Coleridge?"

"Jasmine, go 'way."

"Well, if you ain't, you better say so, 'cause you know how I love ta talk!"

"Who you gonna tell who ain't already heard Leon? You gonna broadcast it to alla your white friends?"

Jasmine smirked. "Shaq's pulling herself up by her shoelaces. Joinin' the suburban *elite*! Tell me, does it feel better when they smarter?"

"Shut your face, Jasmine. I'm doin' nuthin' with nobody. And I wouldn't tell you if I was." I turned my back on her and she went back to her original seat.

I hate having conversations on the bus, which is why I usually bury my face in a book. It's too confusing to speak this home language a few minutes before going into school. I try never to use it in Scrub Harbor. I know some kids stick with it in a proud way, because they like how it sets them apart from the white kids, but I don't like being classified by it. A black girl from Spaulding is not the only thing I am or intend to be.

So I speak two languages: home language, black language, Ebonics, whatever you want to call it, and school language, white English, Nelson's English. But going from one to the other too rapidly makes me feel dizzy. I use the bus like Superman used his telephone booth, as a place to hide while I change into my other identity.

The tin can pulled into the circular drive and the doors opened with a *whoosh,* like when you open a jar and even the air can't wait to get out. We'd all been sitting so long it was hard to drag out of the seats and stumble down the stairs. Eight o'clock in the morning and it felt like the day should be half over already. As usual, we had barely enough time to get to our lockers before first period started, but that was all right with me. I was here for the education, not the social life.

Everybody else was already in Ms. Capshaw's English class when I got there. She smiled at me, as always, and, as always, I wondered if she smiled at everybody as they walked in. Since I was always last, it wasn't likely I'd ever know the answer, but I hoped she did.

My seat is near the back, so it's easy to do a quick check on Nelson, who, wouldn't you guess, sits right up front. He didn't seem to be paying any attention to me, but then, he wouldn't do it obviously. If he looked later I'd be able to tell, even if I seemed to be busy or turned the other way. I could always sense if a boy I liked was looking at me. Not that, in this case, I would do a thing about it.

Ms. Capshaw clapped her hands. "Okay, every-body. Listen up. Gretchen has asked me if she can make a brief announcement before class to-day. Gretchen?"

Gretchen Carstenson slid out of her seat and walked purposefully to the front of the room. This will crack you up, but I have always felt sorry for this girl. How's that for crazy? I mean, she's got more money than Ted Turner, and those white boys seem to love the Goldilocks look she's got going. But something isn't right. She's always standing up and announcing something, trying to be in charge of everything, but I just don't buy it. You look in her eyes and you see she'd rather just be sittin' in the back of the room, like me, just gettin' on with it. Even when she smiles it looks like somebody's standing behind her pulling the strings.

"Okay, you all know what this is about. Last night the selectmen set a date for the vote. It will be November 24, the day before Thanksgiving break." Two or three people clapped. Gretchen kept glancing at the paper in her hand as though she might forget her little speech. She leaned forward and looked right into people's eyes, which made her seem like a bad actress trying to keep your attention during a boring play by being very, very serious.

"So what I need right away is some people to

help me get out the vote. We've got two weeks and I really think going door-to-door is more effective than just handing out flyers. Also, I need some people to hold signs at the polling places on voting day. You won't be excused from school—it'll be either before classes or after."

"How come *we* have to do it?" somebody yelled from the back of the class.

Gretchen gave the joker this tense smile. "You don't *have* to. But the seniors have been the ones most involved in the effort—I guess because so many of them are my friends—so I thought I'd save time by asking in my classes first."

"I have a question." I looked around. It was the new kid, Adam something. He always had to get in his two cents. I had the feeling he was kind of a big deal at his old school and he was trying hard to regain that status here. Somebody should tell him it's too late. These townies are one tight clan—no way this blond bigmouth was gonna worm his way into the inner circle in his senior year.

Ms. Capshaw nodded in his direction.

"Well, it seems like you're just assuming that everyone in here is in favor of the name change. But that might not be the case."

"You don't have to be in favor of the change to be in favor of a vote!" Gretchen said brightly.

"But it seems to me that people who'd rather

keep the name the same have no reason to favor a vote. They've got the name they want now." Adam looked up at her like he thought she'd throw him a biscuit for being so smart.

Ms. Capshaw interrupted. "That's true. But I don't think Gretchen expects everyone to help out. Those who don't want to, certainly don't have to."

But Adam wasn't giving up. "I'm just wondering if people might feel some pressure to do it, since so many of the kids in the honors classes seem to favor it."

All of a sudden everybody wanted to have their say.

"That's because we see the economic benefit of it," Nick Cross said. "It doesn't matter as much to the other kids."

Elle Bennett turned around and glared at Adam. "Nobody's pressuring anybody. It's obvious who's against us anyway!"

"Who's 'us,' Elle? Everybody whose father makes half a million dollars a year?" That was Tim Evans, whose father, I happen to know, is a mail carrier.

Even Nadia Kazirenko, who never says boo, was making these puffing noises through her nose, letting her anger out, I guess, in little sneezes.

Ms. Capshaw interrupted them. "Class! Obviously this is an issue that many of you have strong opinions about. We can take a few minutes to debate it, but not like this, not attacking one another personally."

But it was hard for people to settle down. Tim pounded on his desk. "I know I'm in the minority in here, but I'm a Scrub and I'm proud of it. Most of the Follys weren't even born here. Your parents moved here so you could get a decent education in our schools. And now you want to change everything!"

"Where do you get that?" Nick said. "My grandparents were born here! My father developed all the land behind Baker's Field. If it wasn't for him this place would still be a backwater."

"If it wasn't for him, we'd still have wetlands in back of Baker's Field and more nesting areas for seabirds."

Ms. Capshaw put a stop to it then, but not before the two sides were yelling stuff back and forth about "you Scrubs" and "you Follys" like the two names were the worst curse words they could come up with. I just had to laugh, to tell you the truth. I laughed louder than I've ever laughed in this school the whole time I've been going here. That actually stopped the fighting as much as Ms. Capshaw's yelling did. People turned around and looked at me like they'd forgotten I was even in this class and why the hell was I laughing at their big, important argument? Nelson turned around too, but I was pretty sure he hadn't forgotten I was there.

• • •

"Mind if I sit here?" Nelson was holding his tray of pink ravioli and microwaved corn kernels in front of him, not daring to set it down on my table until I gave the go-ahead.

I looked around. Jasmine had already taken notice. Nothing to do about that. My first year or so here I used to eat lunch with some of the other program kids, even Jasmine herself, but I got tired of it. Always the same group, talking about the same stuff, arguing real loud and enjoying how the white kids stared, but then complaining about it afterward. And eating with the white kids was even worse—I only tried that once. They all talk about football games and play rehearsals and stuff I just can't imagine wasting two minutes of my life on.

So now I usually get here early enough to claim one of the small corner tables for myself and a good friend, like Toni Morrison or Alice Walker or Audre Lord. Lately I'd been reading this autobiography by a man named Henry Louis Gates, an African American who teaches at guess what college? I slipped the book onto my lap and looked up at Nelson.

"It's not about going out. I just want to talk to you a minute."

"Fine," I said, motioning him to a chair. "Talk away."

He settled himself in, but kept his eyes on his lunch as he began to talk. "I'm sorry about Saturday. I know I came off like some know-it-all jerk . . ."

"Nothing to be sorry for," I told him. "You were being you and I was being me, that's all. We just don't have much in common, Nelson. Skin color is not the only thing."

He nodded, then actually looked at me. "I know that. But who *do* we have things in common with? You're not much like the other program kids. I'm not much like the other Scrub Harbor kids."

"Maybe not. But we're more like them than we are like each other."

"I don't think so."

"Well, I do."

Kind of an impasse thing going on there. We were both silent for a minute and then Nelson said, "You have secrets, don't you? I feel like there's a lot you don't tell people. Or at least, you don't tell me."

"Like what?" I gave a little laugh, but it didn't throw him off track.

"Like about Lou Hillyard. I've been remembering some things. You were pretty good friends with him. But for some reason you don't want to tell me why he's in jail."

I sighed. "God, Nelson, why are you so obsessed with Lou Hillyard?"

"I'm not," he said. I could tell he came close to saying more, maybe saying who he *was* obsessed with. I was thankful he managed to hold his tongue.

So I told him the whole story. What difference did it make anyway? I wasn't betraying Lou—he probably wouldn't even remember who Nelson was by now. Maybe he wouldn't even remember who I was since I hadn't been to visit him in over a year.

"You're right, Lou and I were friends. As a matter of fact, the year he went back to Spaulding, our sophomore year, he was my boyfriend."

Nelson had this funny look on his face. "*Good* friends," he said.

"Yeah, good friends. We were both having a hard time trying to figure out where we belonged. It was hell coming out here to school every day. *Hell.* But it was even worse staying in Spaulding where just about everybody had given up. We argued about that a lot, whether he should come back to Scrub Harbor or I should go to Spaulding, but neither of us would change."

"So then what? He started doing drugs?" I

could see Nelson was eager to get to the part where I'd start trashing Lou.

I shook my head. "Lou was never using. It was my brother, Darius, who started him dealing. He'd dropped out of school and he needed money. We all needed money; you got to have money to live, even in Spaulding. Darius could never have gotten a job that paid as well as dealing, even with a high school diploma. Lou saw that and he asked Darius to get him started."

"This is your brother? The one you were trying to find on Saturday?"

"That's the one."

Nelson leaned over and put his hand on my arm. "Shaquanda, if he's dealing drugs you can't be involved with him. You need to cut him loose. Let him take care of himself. You can't be responsible—"

I shook off his hand. "Nelson, are you listening to me? Darius takes care of *us*! My mother works nights cleaning office buildings. Do you think she makes enough money to feed four children and pay rent?"

"Your family's living on drug money?"

"On whatever money there is. How many program kids drop out before their senior year? Why am I so lucky not to have to quit school and look for work? Because Darius gives us money—maybe

it's from gambling, maybe it's from girls, maybe
it's from drugs—I don't ask where he gets it."

Nelson was quiet, but he was staring at me.

"You heard enough secrets?" I asked him.

"No. You didn't finish telling me about Lou.
Why is he in jail?"

"He got caught dealing. Twice. Second time
he got two years. He should be getting out just
about the time we graduate from Scrub Harbor
High."

Nelson nodded. "That's convenient. Is that
why you don't date anyone? Because you're waiting for him to get out?"

Now that was actually funny. "I don't date anyone because I don't have the time. I study, I take
care of my little sisters, I ride the bus. If I'm
lucky, there's some time left over to sleep."

"So, you aren't waiting for Lou?"

I shrugged. "When people go to jail, you
never know who's gonna come out at the end. He
was a good guy, but he won't be the same. Somebody told me he takes art classes and draws my
picture from a photograph he's got. If that's true,
I hope it's because he's practicing to be an artist
when he gets out. I hope he doesn't have plans
that include me, because my plans don't include
anybody but myself."

Nelson nodded. "I got it."

I was hoping he'd get up and leave. I can talk

so hard it scares people sometimes, but right underneath that I almost feel like I'm crying at the same time. Which is how I felt sitting there with Nelson, who is such a good person you feel kind of shabby by comparison. If I lived in Scrub Harbor and I had a father who carried mail or did any regular kind of thing, and Darius had gone off to college already, and my mother worked part-time in the school office to pay his way—if we were poor like *that*, I think I could open up my heart to this boy. But we're from Spaulding, which might as well be on the moon.

I guess I laughed again. The kind of laugh when things are ironic more than funny.

Nelson pointed his finger at my face. "Every time you laugh like that it's another secret I'll never know, isn't it? You're laughing at something nobody knows but you. Like this morning in Ms. Capshaw's class. When everybody else was having that knockdown argument and you started hooting. What was that all about?"

I shook my head. "Eat your ravioli, Nelson. You don't wanna know."

"The ravioli is toxic. And you know I want to know. Tell me."

The boy does not give up, which I guess is why he's Number Two in the class. So I told him: "It just struck me funny the way you were all screaming at each other. *The Follys are in honors classes*

*and the Scrubs aren't! The Scrubs have lived here
for two hundred years and the Follys haven't. The
Follys are rich and the Scrubs aren't!* As though
there's a teaspoonful of difference between alla
you people!"

"Are you kidding? There are huge differences!"

"Nelson," I said straight out. "No matter what
you think of yourselves, you're all a bunch of
Follys to me."

He sat up very straight in his chair, like I'd
slapped him. "Well, thanks a lot. I guess that puts
me in my place." He stood up and grabbed his
tray, strode across the cafeteria, and dumped the
contents onto a conveyer belt that took his un-
touched food back to the kitchen to be tossed.
My heart was pounding a little, seeing him so
angry, and knowing I'd made it happen. I looked
away.

I had just sneaked my book back up onto the
table, trying to knock Nelson out of my head so I
could go back to being alone again, when I realized he was coming back toward me. Before I
could do more than flip the cover closed, he was
leaning over the table.

"I just wanted to tell you something you might
not have been aware of," he said. "That book
you're reading by Henry Louis Gates . . ."

Damn. I knew what was coming.

". . . he teaches at Harvard."

I didn't say a word.

"So, you think everybody at Harvard is a Folly, too? You think there's nothing a Folly could teach you?" he asked me.

I let the question simmer a minute, then decided not to deal with it. "I don't know," I said. I slipped the book off the table and into my pack; I hoped Nelson couldn't tell that touching it made my fingers burn.

"No, you don't know," he said right back at me. "Too bad you never will."

It was the first time I'd ever heard Nelson say anything mean.

Adam

As usual I came right home after school and went online. *You've got mail!* the voice said, ready as always to announce the good news. I clicked on the mailbox and sure enough, all the usual suspects were accounted for: ConanLove, Phantacorn, Bump43, Hankerous. Most of my old crowd from Bishops Hill. Not WaterbabeX though. Hadn't heard from her since our disastrous phone call last week. Hey, no biggie. I'm here, she's there; it had to happen. Like I'm so surprised Teddy Halloran swooped in for the kill two minutes after the moving van left town. (Although I must admit I expected Mara to hold out for more than a weepy week or two before leaping into the arms of some hairball like Ted.)

My other friends have been loading up my mailbox about it all week.

ConanLove (Sarah): *Adam, I swear I had no idea. How could she do this to you?*

Phantacorn (Phil): *Like they say on the* X-Files: *Trust No One.*

Bump43 (Claudia): *You don't need her, Adam. The girls in that swanky suburb are probably dropping dead at your feet already. Right?*

Hankerous (Hank): *I can't believe she'd go out with Halloran and not ME.*

Mara and I probably would have broken up at the end of the year anyway, after the prom and everything. Everybody knows it's a bad idea to go off to college without saying bye-bye to your high school honey. It's too hard to be faithful long distance. Who wants to? And this is practically the same thing.

The only problem is I'm not *in* college. I'm in a high school where everybody else already made their friends ten years ago and they aren't that interested in enlarging their circle the year before they all split up anyway. I wondered if my friends and I would have acted the same way if there had been a new kid in our class senior year, some smart-ass like me who thought he was good enough to be our friend. Not out of the realm of possibility.

But hey, I'm not freaking. I mean, it's one year. I left one year earlier than the rest of my class, that's all. Dad has been hoping for this transfer forever; I'm not going to make a big stink about it. I had been planning to go back to Bishops Hill to visit, probably take Mara to the prom and all. Whatever. That won't happen. Sarah would probably go with me though, if I wanted her to.

The funny thing is, the kids in Scrub Harbor aren't all that different from the kids in Bishops Hill, except that the kids here don't know me. They don't know about how I've always had a million friends. They don't know about how last year I cocaptained the math team and the basketball team, which both won divisional titles in the same week. They don't know how often I've been on Student Council, or how many fund-raisers I've been in charge of, or how the girls I wanted always seemed to want me back. I guess the big surprise is how that stuff doesn't stick to you once you leave a place. It makes me feel like I'm not the same person I was in Bishops Hill. I mean, if I am, why don't they see it? Maybe we're only who other people think we are (in which case all I have to do is change the way these people think).

There's a girl here who reminds me of Mara. Blond, energetic, in charge of everything. She goes with this big jock who stands there admiring her while she runs around telling everybody what to do. Maybe it's because Mara just dumped me, but I'm finding this Gretchen person very annoying. On the other hand, she's damn good-looking.

The whole town is having a big debate right now about whether or not to change its name from

what it was always called to a fancier name that the
rich people like better. Seems kind of silly to me.
It's still the same place no matter what you call it.
Gretchen seems to be leading the charge for the
name change. I keep thinking about how Grandma
used to say, *If it ain't broke, don't fix it.* It seems
like that might apply to this situation.

Actually I'm the one who seems to be broken,
sitting here every afternoon scribbling E-mail
messages to people hundreds of miles away, all of
whom have better things to do than answer me.
And before much longer, they'll probably be
doing those better things. So, if I'm not going to
have a totally crummy senior year, I better get off
my butt and fix things. Now.

• • •

The beachfront in Scrub Harbor is pretty amaz-
ing. When we arrived here Dad drove into town
on the shore road, figuring we'd be impressed by
the wide sandy curve that cups around the
Atlantic Ocean and the clapboard houses and
white church steeples rising up the short hills just
beyond the boardwalk. Mom acted just a little too
thrilled, I thought, for someone who'd just left
behind a thriving antiques business and her best
friend since high school.

She really wanted me to buy into the excite-
ment too. "Look, Adam, the town's right on the

ocean. I bet the local kids have picnics down there in nice weather." I tried to imagine hanging out on the beach, making bonfires and roasting hot dogs with friends, swimming in the summer, maybe getting a wet suit and learning to surf on the baby waves. *Maybe it'll turn out to be great,* I thought. *Maybe I've just landed in the middle of* Baywatch *and don't even know it!*

Hah! That was weeks ago and I haven't even walked on the sand yet. To tell you the truth, I kind of forgot it was there. The beautiful view is nowhere near our house and I don't take that route to school, which is about the only place I ever go. But instead of spending yet another afternoon on the computer writing tales of misery to half the population of Bishops Hill, Vermont, I decided to go down to the beach and check it out.

The tide was low when I got down there, and the breeze off the water made me zip up my coat even though the sun felt warm. I walked from one end of the long beach to the other, teasing the little breakers and getting my sneakers wet. Then I realized that when the water was out that far you could follow the beach around a promontory of rock that otherwise stuck way out into the water. There was a smaller beach on the other side, more private, with rock outcroppings all around the perimeter.

What a spot. The promontory cut off the

worst of the wind and it was warm, especially sitting down on the sand. I found a flat rock to lean against and took off my shoes and socks so I could feel the gritty itch of the sand on my feet. It was the happiest moment I'd had since I got here. I was sitting there thinking, *Okay, here's one big plus: There are no beaches like this in Bishops Hill.* It was so beautiful and peaceful sitting there looking at the faraway waves spilling in and breaking on the shore, then racing each other across the wet sand.

There were a few houses built up on top of the rocks. Big brick houses, with huge decks and porches and glassed-in greenhouses extending out on all sides. The people who lived there probably never forgot the ocean; they could have this view right from their living-room couches. It didn't look right though, such big houses sitting up on those rocks, butting themselves into nature. It didn't seem quite fair that somebody could buy the sky and the cliffs and the Atlantic Ocean that way.

I put my face up so I could feel the sun beat down on it. This was not the kind of thing I'd ever do at home. In Vermont, I mean. For one thing, I was almost never alone there, and I was always *doing* something. I never just sat somewhere and looked around and enjoyed the place. Maybe I'd be a different person this year. Why

not? My Scrub Harbor year. I'd be more thoughtful. I could buy a journal. And come out here
every afternoon and sit on the beach and think
and write and appreciate things.

The more I thought about it, moving here
started to feel like it could be an opportunity.
How many times had I wished I didn't have to go
to some meeting or party or movie, but all my
friends were going and I couldn't just say I didn't
want to. We did everything together, like some
hive or flock going on instinct: time to work on
the yearbook, time to plan the prom, time to run
for office, time to make the honey, time to fly
south for the winter.

If I could just make one good friend here, that
would be all I'd need. Maybe a girl, but maybe
not. Somebody with a mind of her own, like that
Nadia, who'd be content to sit quietly on the
beach and contemplate the sun as it dropped into
the ocean. That's all the new Adam would need
to be happy here, I was sure.

I heard the yapping sound before I saw anything. It sounded like one of those cheap radio-
controlled cars everybody had when we were about
eight years old, but I knew those wouldn't run on
sand. And then it was standing right in front of me,
this funny-looking little dog with his belly dragging
in the sand, gargling his lungs.

"Hey, who are you?" I put my hand down,

palm up, so he could smell me and not be afraid. He gave one more little bark and peed in the sand.

"Patty! You idiot!" Someone was chasing after the dog. "Stop! If you eat seaweed again . . ."

By the time she came around the corner of the rock I was leaning against, little Patty was sitting in my lap, licking my chin. I'm not sure which of us was more surprised.

"You!" Gretchen said. "What are you doing here?"

"Actually, not a damn thing," I said. "Care to join me?"

She looked flustered. "Patty, get off him."

"He's not bothering me. Or she. Patty?"

She crossed her arms in front of her tightly, like she was double locking the door. "Pattypan Squash. Don't look at me, he's my mother's dog. I only walk him when she makes me. Which is as little as possible since he doesn't listen to me." She brushed her hair out of her eyes.

"Cute dog," I said. He wasn't really very cute, but, due to my mother's allergies, I've never been able to have a dog so I like almost all of them, even ratty-looking old guys like this one.

"Ha, ha. I can't believe he's sitting in your lap like that. He hates humans."

"Oh, well, see, that's the thing. I'm an extra-terrestrial."

Barely a smirk. "Right."

"Where's your bodyguard?"

"My *what*? Oh, you mean Quincy. Very funny."

Her sense of humor didn't seem to be overly developed. "If you say so. I've hardly ever seen you without him hovering nearby."

"He has football practice after school." She was pawing the sand with her sneaker like an angry bull.

I nodded. "So, can you sit down a few minutes?"

She looked up and down the beach like she thought somebody was following her. "I've got stuff to do."

"Yeah, I know you're a busy person," I said.

She plunked herself down cross-legged about five feet away from me, so I wouldn't get the idea she was too friendly, I guess. "There's usually nobody down here," she said.

"Why not? It's a great place."

"Well, technically it's private property."

"You're kidding."

"Nope. This part. Above the high tide mark. But in the winter nobody cares. It's only in the summer people get chased off."

"But it's the ocean! How can somebody own it?"

"Technically this is Folly Bay, although, of course, it's ocean water, but it's sheltered here in the harbor."

"Scrub Harbor," I said, smiling. "Technically."

I was goading her a little, I admit. But she was so stiff and self-righteous, she was reminding me more and more of Mara, the betrayer.

She didn't say anything for a minute, but I knew I must have hit a bull's-eye because her mouth drew up into a knot and she pulled her knees in close enough to hug.

"I suppose you're against us too," she said finally, then sighed and let her shoulders sag. "I don't know how this got so crazy. It seemed like a good idea when my mother told me about it; it was just to give the town a more attractive name. I never thought it would be such a big deal, but now it's splitting everybody into groups: rich, poor, Scrubs, Follys, oceanfronters, and back-siders. Everybody's calling each other names. I hate it. And I feel like it's *my fault*."

She turned away and I knew she was probably whisking away an unruly tear she'd be horrified for me to see. I felt bad for joking about it, but who would have suspected Ms. Cool and Aloof would be having a crisis over this?

"Hey," I said, "I'm new here. I'm not taking sides. It doesn't matter to me one way or the other."

"It doesn't really matter to me either!" she said. "That's the stupid thing. I've always loved Scrub Harbor." She threw one arm out toward the water. "*And* Folly Bay. They're the same place to me, where the land and sea come together. I thought changing the name was a good idea—I didn't know people would get so mad about it!"

Pattypan was whining. "I think you're scaring your dog."

Gretchen threw the hound a glare. "He ought to be used to it. My mother is constantly raving about this too. Except she's mostly mad that people think she's just doing it to sell more real estate." She stared off into the sea. "Which might be true."

I thought a slight change of topic might be in order. "Why was the town called Scrub Harbor in the first place?"

She was sullen now, drawing circles in the sand with a stick. "There used to be a big grove of scrub pine up on that hill. But it was cut down ages ago."

"Where? You mean up there where that monstrosity of a house is?" I pointed toward the glassed-in, decked-out brick thing that teetered on the rock.

Gretchen looked up suddenly, following my gesture. She looked at the house for a minute, as if she'd never noticed it before, then said, "Yeah, right there. Where my house is. They cut down the pine to build our monstrosity and a couple of others like it."

Nobody said anything for a few minutes while I tried to get my size twelve foot out of my big mouth. Finally I said, "So, this beach I'm trespassing on is probably *yours*?"

She smiled then, but not at me, just into the wind. "Technically. But since you're such a good friend of Pattypan's we won't chase you off. I swear I've never seen that mutt take to anybody like that. I'm telling you, he hates *everybody*." Patty had curled up in my lap, his nose stuck underneath my hand.

"Well, I think the thing that's happened here is that for some reason everything that has to do with me is reversed. Just the opposite of what it used to be. Even Patty here. I'm caught in the Twilight Zone or a Stephen King novel or something. My friend Phil would be waiting for Mulder and Scully to arrive momentarily. Nothing is the way it should be, or the way I thought it would be."

She was confused. "You mean nothing in Scrub Harbor is the way you thought it would be? Because it's so different from the place you lived before?"

"No. It's actually not that different. I mean, it looks different—there's no ocean in Bishops Hill—but the people are pretty much the same. I'm just not one of them. Of you. So, it's weird. Kind of an out-of-body experience."

"I'm not sure what you mean," she said.

I knew I was telling the wrong person these

things. I should have been confiding to some strong individualist like Nadia, but I'd managed to get on her bad side right off the bat. She would have understood this though, I was pretty sure.

"Believe it or not, I was popular in Bishops Hill," I said. "Real popular. Whatever that means. I hung out with the kids who thought quite a lot of themselves. We were cool—we were the rulers of the school, the kings and queens. But that's not who I'm going to be here. I don't *know* who I'm going to be here, which is a strange feeling. The invisible man."

She looked uncomfortable. "I guess it's hard to come here in your senior year. Everybody's kind of settled with their friends . . ."

I nodded. "I know. I would have felt the same way if I'd stayed in Bishops Hill and somebody new showed up there. *Leave me alone—I don't have time to get to know some new guy.* But now that I'm here I'm thinking maybe I was a big jerk."

"You think the kids here are jerks?" She didn't sound too upset about the possibility.

"No more than kids anyplace else. I'm not really thinking about them that much. I'm just trying to figure out who I am, you know? Maybe I don't want to be the same person I was before. I mean, *can* I be somebody else?"

Gretchen was actually looking at me now, although I wasn't sure what she was seeing. "Do you think you can?"

"Well, I'm kind of being forced to. But maybe that's good."

She nodded. "I'm sick of being popular."

I was so surprised I didn't say anything. I think she was surprised she'd said it too. She laughed nervously. "Don't ever tell anybody I said that! I mean, it sounds awful, like I'm really conceited or something."

"I think I know what you mean," I said. "After a while popularity is like some terrible creature you have to keep on feeding or it kills you."

She jumped up onto her knees. "That's right! Sometimes I feel like popularity created me and now I have to do what it wants. I have to be who everybody expects a popular girl to be. Sometimes I just don't want to. Sometimes I wish I could go to school without washing my hair or finishing my homework or talking to anybody all day long."

"To get out of your own skin for a while."

"Yeah!"

It was her smile, shining out beneath that blond hair, that really reminded me of Mara. Which was too bad, because that memory, the smile-memory, still hurt.

She was still smiling when I asked her, "Do

you know a girl named Nadia in the senior class?"

She wasn't expecting that question. "Um, yeah. Nadia Kazirenko. She's Russian."

"From Russia, yeah, that's her. She's a person who seems to have a good sense of herself. I'd like to be as confident of who I am as she is."

"What?" Now Gretchen's laugh had a nasty edge to it that I recognized—a laugh to remind me who I was talking to. "Confident? The Nadia I know follows Nelson Coleridge around like a ghost; I've hardly ever heard her speak above a whisper. She's just *odd*." She got to her feet and brushed the sand off the back of her jeans. I guess if I was talking about another girl she was ending the conversation.

"She's interesting. You probably don't really know her very well. Have you ever really talked to her?"

"No, I suppose I haven't. Really, Adam, there just isn't *time* to be friends with every single person."

She knew my name; I'd been wondering.

"It's getting late," she said. "I've got to get home. Wouldn't want Patty to be late for dinner."

I stood too, handing her her pooch, who immediately struggled to get down. "I've got to go too. Private beach, you know."

"You can use it whenever you want." She looked up the hill toward her house, as though someone might be watching her. "Let me show you how to come when the tide's in, when you can't come around the rock from the public beach."

"Are you supposed to show me? I might turn out to be a Scrub." It was a joke, but a little mean under the circumstances.

"You can bring your friend Nadia," she said, "unless she's afraid of dogs." I followed her through the space between two rocks and then we turned in different directions.

• • •

"There you are," Mom said when I came through the kitchen door. "I'm glad you didn't spend the whole afternoon in your room on such a nice day."

"I was down at the beach. It's pretty here, isn't it?"

"Gorgeous!" she said, overcompensating as usual.

"How was your day? Meet anybody interesting?" I asked her.

"I did actually. Interviewed for two jobs. One was in a shop run by a nice young woman. I think I could get along with her." Such a glowing recommendation. Mom's transition wasn't going much better than mine.

I'd give her a little gift. "I met a girl from school down on the beach."

Big smile. "Why am I not surprised? Adam Russell strikes again!"

It was important to her, who I was. Maybe more now than in Bishops Hill where she had other things on her mind and an interesting life of her own.

She stopped chopping eggplant and turned to talk. "Details? Who is she? Do you like her?"

In Bishops Hill I would have said, "Sure, I like her. I like *all* girls, Mom. You know that!" And she would have laughed, certain that all things were as they should be. But all things had suddenly fallen apart. And I wasn't ready yet to figure out the way they might fit back together in Scrub Harbor.

"I don't really know her," I said. "Besides, she looks too much like Mara. Don't get your hopes up."

That surprised her. She turned back to her vegetables without a word. Poor Mom. Her hopes are always up; they've got no place to go but down.

Quincy

I'm the kind of guy who doesn't like change. Never have. I like things to keep going along the way they are. Mom pointed out to me once that I never break up with my girlfriends. Even if I'm tired of a girl and thinking how I'd like to go out with somebody else, I wait until she says it's over, and then I feel kind of bad about it. I guess I'm thinking about this now because things aren't so good with Gretchen lately. She used to think I was the greatest thing since potato chips in a can, which made me think she was pretty great too, but for some reason we aren't connecting like that anymore.

We never had much in common. She was always running a political campaign or getting petitions signed or something. I was sort of impressed by that—how smart she was and how she always had "important" stuff to do. She's one of those girls who has the whole package: beauty, brains, popularity. But I can't get behind this whole Folly Bay business—like I said, I don't like change. I go to her meetings and help her hand out flyers and stuff, but I guess she thinks I'm letting her down by not being too gung ho about it.

And that's not the only thing going on. Last week O'Neill posted that damn poem he wrote on the main bulletin board outside the principal's office. Most of the kids had already read it by the time Flanders figured out what it was about and took it down. Then that Christine Muser (why is this *her* business?) suggested O'Neill post it *again,* in case anybody missed it the first time. Which turned him into some kind of rebel saint for all the hopeless cases at Scrub Harbor High School and also got him a week's worth of detention.

Man, I've never run the track as fast as I'm running it today. Like somebody's chasing me. Coach gave us the afternoon off, but I'm too hyped up to just sit around. I could forget everything doing this, running around and around the oval, except that every now and then I see some guy standing there tying his shoelaces or something, just waiting for me to run past so he can stare at me, to see if I've sprouted horns or fangs or something, I guess. To see how I'm *handling* it.

"Quincy!"

Here she is, coming to harangue me. I'm not doing this the way she wants me too. I'm not *coming to grips with it* the way she thinks I should. Why do I have to handle or grip anything? It's not my problem.

I slow down as I approach her, motioning for her to join me as I walk it out. It's funny. I look at Gretchen now and I hardly even see how pretty she is. I mean I know she's still pretty, but now when I look at her all I can see is that she's not satisfied with me. It's hard to feel great about somebody who's pissed off at you.

"So, are you going to the meeting? It starts in five minutes," she says. Like we haven't already talked about this.

"Look," I say, panting at her. It's hard to hold a conversation when you've been running hard for twenty minutes. "There's no point. He doesn't need me there."

"Q, he *asked* you to go."

"He didn't *ask* me. He left a notice for the meeting in my car."

"He's your brother. There's not even a practice today—you have no excuse!"

"Why the hell do I need an excuse?" I say. "I'm taking a shower—that's my excuse. But you go, if you want. Take notes."

"I think you should go for *you,* Quincy, not just for O'Neill."

"Christ, Gretchen. Don't try to shrink me, okay?"

"I'm not shrinking you."

I remember a topic I'd much rather talk about. "You know what? I'm almost finished editing my video for my TV production class. I want to show you—"

"You're changing the subject."

"No, listen. I think you'll like it. I interviewed twenty-eight kids about smoking: how they got started, if their parents smoked, if they thought about the health risks . . ." I'm starting to get excited remembering what good footage I got, how Mr. Wiesner thinks I should enter it in this contest—

"Quincy, I'm trying to talk to you about something *important*," Gretchen says.

I just glare at her for a minute. "Oh, excuse me. How stupid of me to think there might be something important going on in *my* life too."

She just lets out this big sigh, like she has so much to put up with and now there's the burden of *me*, too. So I leave her standing outside the locker room door, knowing that entering my hideout in midconversation won't be a big help to our relationship.

Only another athlete would understand how walking into that steamy, stinky den charges me up. I know it's sort of a joke, that *manly man* thing, but I really do like the feeling of being with other guys who do sports, who use their

bodies and take pride in them. To be a good athlete: It's not nothing.

There are a couple of guys already in the
shower, these two wrestlers who were in the
weight room. Jack and Somebody. I don't really
know them—they're younger. I strip down and
step in under the spray, saying hey, the way you
do, not really paying much attention to them. I
know they know who I am. I'm a senior, after all,
and cocaptain of the football team.

They finish up pretty fast and leave me in the
mist by myself. I can hear them talking though,
and as soon as I get out Jack says, "Is O'Neill Sayers your brother?"

I don't answer right away. I open my locker
and start to towel off. "Yeah," I tell him, trying
not to put a question mark at the end of it, pretending I don't know what's coming next.

"Is it true?" he says. "I mean, did you know
about it?"

"You from the *National Enquirer*?" I say,
thinking maybe I can joke my way through this.

Not a grin from the wrestlers; they wait
silently for my answer. Do I have to talk about
this all the time now? I'm just the brother.

"I guess it's true," I tell them. "Why would he
lie about it?"

The first thing I thought of after I read the
poem (which, by the way, was really fun: finding

out my only brother is gay in front of a dozen giggling morons) was that time O'Neill came home
from, I don't know, probably eighth grade, all
upset because some girl had followed him into
the woods and tried to kiss him. I couldn't believe it: I'd been praying some girl would actually allow me to put my lips on hers, and here
my little brother was getting it handed to him
on a plate and he was freaking out. At the time I
just thought he was a dweeb, too dopey to take
advantage of a good thing. Of course, looking
back now . . .

"So you didn't suspect anything? I mean,
other than the obvious stuff."

"What obvious stuff?" This jerk is starting to
annoy me.

Jack puts his hands in front of him. "No
offense. I just meant, you know, he never played
sports or anything, like you. He's more, like,
quiet. Gets good grades."

Jesus, it's guys like this that give athletes a bad
name. "Yeah, his grades were the real tip-off," I
tell them. "All these honor students are queer—
didn't you know that?"

They turn away from me then, but I'm the
kind of guy that, I don't get mad fast, but once I
do, I don't just get over it right away.

"Where'd you get your brains, Jack, from a

toxic-waste dump? Where the hell do you get off asking me personal questions, like you're my goddamn best friend?"

I guess they aren't crazy about having some buck-naked senior yelling at them. They get their crap together and leave fast. By the time I get dressed I'm actually feeling a little nauseous. I can see this is just the beginning. I'm going to be fighting this thing for a while whether I want to or not. O'Neill might be having a great time at his coming-out party, but I'm not so crazy about *my* new identity: the football player with the in-your-face gay brother. Maybe when people give me sideways glances in the hall now, they're wondering, *Is he gay too?* Thanks, bro.

It occurs to me that if I'm getting this much attention, O'Neill must really feel like he's under a microscope. But he didn't have to announce it, did he? He's kept it secret this long, why not wait until after high school to tell people?

It might have been easier on Mom that way too. She's been lying around the house all week like a balloon without air. O'Neill didn't even tell her himself. She found out about it from her tennis partner whose daughter saw the poem on the bulletin board. (I guess I could have told her, but I couldn't figure out how. She thinks O'Neill is so frigging perfect.) When she asked him if the poem was some kind of a joke, he said, "If so, it's not very funny, is it?" Do you get points for telling the truth if it hurts people?

I guess Dad isn't losing any sleep over it. He says it's just a phase, O'Neill showing off or something, being different. But that's Dad. He's not too good at dealing with hard stuff. If Mom's mad at him, it's time to take a business trip. If I flunk chemistry, it's time to introduce me to his old football buddy who owns a chain of electronics stores. ("He wasn't Ivy League material either, but he's a wealthy man now!") If O'Neill is gay, it's time to look at those viewbooks from Yale and Princeton. Dad won't sit in front of the TV crying over *My So-Called Life* reruns like Mom.

I start to go out the back door, but why should I walk around the whole building just to avoid passing the room where they hold that silly meeting? It's probably over already anyway. From what I hear the Gay/Straight Alliance is mostly straight girls (and a few who say they're bisexual) getting together to watch movies about gay guys. Hey, whatever turns you on, I guess. They're all probably thrilled to latch onto O'Neill—finally they've got a real live homosexual! Of course, they have Tompkins, that queer English teacher, but really, how many high school guys are gonna fess up to being gay?

Oh, my God. There are so many people at the

meeting, they're crammed in the doorway, trying to see over other people's heads. I can't believe it! There are even guys from the football team, who I know damn well are not here to pop out of the closet. They want to see what's going to happen next. They want to see Quincy Sayers's brother make an ass of himself!

I'm the kind of guy who, though I may not get along that great with my brother, I'm sure as hell not putting up with anybody else screwing with him. *I* can take a shot at the guy, but you better not try it.

So I edge up to the back of the crowd. I can see over the heads of most of the kids in the doorway, and a few of them back off when they see who it is and let me get a little farther in. There's O'Neill sitting over by the windows with Christine in front of him and Gretchen behind him, his new groupies. I didn't even think Gretchen liked him all that much. He was always just as snotty to her as he was to me. What is it with girls? They're all crazy to *help* everybody. I could probably save our relationship by becoming a crack addict.

Sounds like Tompkins is just finishing up some old business of some kind, something about tickets for an AIDS benefit in Boston. Then he stops and looks around at all the kids sitting on the radiators and hanging in the doorway.

"Well, this is the largest turnout we've ever had

for a GSA meeting. I guess my idea about putting something in the drinking water worked!" His loyal followers laugh hysterically.

"No, no, just kidding. Don't anybody report me to the Health Department. I would like to ask a question though. How many of you are here because you read a poem by O'Neill Sayers that was posted on the bulletin board?"

A bunch of kids raise their hands. They're anxious to admit they're nosy, just in case anybody thought they were there for any other reason.

"Well, that's fine. We're glad to see so many people taking an interest in our group, even if that interest is a little voyeuristic," he says. The standers and slouchers shuffle their feet at that one. Some of them are probably looking around for a dictionary. "O'Neill has asked me if he could say a few words to the group today, since he's a new, but obviously well-known, member. O'Neill?"

My stomach is boiling. What the hell is he going to say now? A few guys look at me quickly, then look away.

O'Neill stands up slowly, where he is, at the side of the room. "I guess a lot of you read my poem," he says, "and now you're here to see if I'm going to self-destruct. Well, don't hold your breath. As weird as this all is, I'm glad I did it." I'm keeping my eyes glued to my brother. I'm pretending my face isn't hotter than a stove. I'm trying to hear what he's saying.

"I don't feel I owe anybody an explanation, but Tompkins . . . *Mr.* Tompkins said if I talked a little bit about why I decided to come out, it might help somebody else. So . . ." He stares up at the ceiling for a minute like maybe his speech is written up there. "The thing is, I always thought the reason I didn't have friends was because I was so different from everybody else. *Better,* is what I thought, to tell you the truth. Sometimes I felt like an alien who'd been dropped on Earth from another planet. Then one day it just hit me that I didn't have any friends because . . . because I was a liar." I don't think it's my imagination that he glances at Christine.

"So, I'm tired of lying. To myself or anybody else. I'm gay. And maybe I'm also an ungrateful child and a lousy brother and a spoiled brat. I don't expect everybody to like me all of a sudden. But at least now, whether you like me or not, you'll know who I am."

O'Neill sits back down as all the hard-core GSA members (and Christine and Gretchen) applaud. Most people just look uncomfortable, like they weren't expecting O'Neill to talk about lying and not having any friends. I think they came to hear the punch line to a joke, only now they don't get it.

I back out of the crowd and walk down the hall, watched, I'm sure, by every kid with eyes. O'Neill wanted me to come to the meeting, and now I think I know why. That thing he said about feeling like an alien dropped onto Earth—that was something I once said to him when we were little kids. I was mad at him for some reason (he's always loved pissing me off) and I told him, "You're weird, O'Neill. You're from another planet. Mom didn't even born you!" I probably wouldn't remember this except that Mom heard me say it and I got sent to my room while O'Neill, the weirdo, got to eat about a hundred chocolate chip cookies.

I wasn't just being mean. He *had* always seemed different from other people. And the explanation he gave that roomful of pop-eyed kids made more sense the longer I thought about it. He *was* always lying. Not lying about who broke the TV or who hit who, not that kind of stuff. Lying about *everything:* what he thought and what he felt and what he wanted. He lied about everything important. It hits me between the eyes like a brick: I don't know who the hell my own brother is.

I drive home feeling foggy. For one thing it's strange not to have Gretchen in the car, talking, talking, talking. Sometimes I can't think around her. She's so smart and she has so many opinions it's just easier to go along with whatever she's saying than to try to get my own thoughts out. I'm surrounded by all these damn geniuses. But today my own ideas are so thick and confusing, they're swirling around my head like flies. Why *didn't* I know it before this?

I'm surprised to see Dad's car in the driveway. He works late more often than not, and almost never comes home this early. But for some reason he's out in the backyard this afternoon raking leaves.

"Doesn't the gardener do that?" I say, coming up behind him.

"Quincy. Good to see you, son." He leans on the rake like it's a crutch. "I needed some busy-work this afternoon. Needed to get up out of my chair and do something physical."

I know what he means by that. "Where's Mom?" I ask.

"Lying down. She's still a little . . . upset."

There aren't enough leaves left to make a respectable pile so Dad's been raking them little by little toward the compost bin in the corner of the yard. There are lines of leaves zigzagging all across the yard, like there wasn't much of a master plan behind the job.

"O'Neill spoke at that meeting this afternoon, Dad."

"Your mother said he intended to."

"Dad. I don't think this is a phase."

He stops raking and leans back against the patio table. "You don't."

"I listened to him. He said he's always felt different. Like an alien."

Dad lets the rake drop, closes his eyes and rubs them with his thumb and first finger. I imagine the fireworks he's setting off against the black background of his eyelids. "Well," he says, "I suppose time will tell. There's not much we can do about it, is there?"

He's quiet for so long, I start to worry. I guess I was wrong about this not bothering him. I've never seen him like this, standing around like some old geezer, not sure what to do next.

Finally I say, "I can see why he had to do it, but I still think he should have waited. This is too hard for you and Mom."

He takes his hand away from his face and gives me a little smile. "When would it have been easier?" he says, then shakes his head and throws his arm around my shoulder. "Quincy, I want to thank you."

"Thank me? What for?"

"For being a good kid. You're the kind of a guy a parent never has to worry about. You're loyal to your friends, you're a hard worker, you get the job done. And if I haven't told you before, I'm proud of you for it."

He leans over and picks up the rake and walks back to the garage with it. I'm stunned. This is too bizarre. I'm being appreciated now because O'Neill is gay? He's dropped down a few notches in the parental ratings so I've surged ahead? Or has Dad always felt this way and just forgotten to mention it because he's usually so busy congratulating O'Neill for being "Ivy League material"?

Why is everybody's opinion of *me* suddenly changing just because my brother is declaring who *he* is? As though, if I'm not his clone I must be his exact opposite.

The guys in the locker room want me to rag on him to prove what a big difference there is between the macho, straight brother and the wimpy, gay one.

Gretchen is so impressed with O'Neill for figuring himself out, but when I try to tell her about my new interest, it's not *important* enough.

Dad's worried about O'Neill now, but he's proud of me because I'm so dependable and boring, he doesn't need to give me a second thought.

Instead of just being me I've suddenly turned into *Not-O'Neill*. And I don't like it.

An hour later I'm in the kitchen when I hear a car pull into the driveway. It's him. I hear him talking to whoever dropped him off and I lean over the sink to see: Christine, grinning so big her cheekbones are pushing up into her ears. That's funny. I always thought she had a thing for O'Neill, but she sure doesn't look broken up about the news.

It's getting dark, but I haven't turned on the lights. When O'Neill comes in I say, "Hi," and he jumps, not seeing me there in the corner.

"God, Quincy. Scare the crap out of me, why don't you?"

"Sorry," I say, smiling.

"I bet." He walks past me, heading for the stairs.

"I've been waiting for you," I tell him.

He sighs and stops, comes back in. "Yeah? You want to critique my speech? I saw you in the doorway. You didn't stay long."

"I heard the important part," I say.

He nods. "Good."

"I just have one question," I say. "Are you sure? I mean, how can you really be *sure*?"

He snickers. "You'll have to take my word for it, Quincy. I'm not giving you any details."

It wasn't details I was after. Just truth. Something that wouldn't change again tomorrow.

"Anyway," he says. "Thanks for coming."

"I wasn't going to at first, but I'm glad I heard what you said. The stuff about you feeling like an alien—was that because I said that to you when we were kids?"

"You said what to me?" He looks confused.

"You know, I called you an alien that time. I said Mom wasn't your mother."

He laughed. "I don't even remember that. You probably did, though. You weren't too nuts about me."

"And vice versa," I say. It's so dark now I can barely see his face. I like talking in the dark. It's easier.

"True," he admits. I can hear him breathing, or maybe it's just me. "So, Quincy, do you hate having a gay brother?"

I make a face, but he can't see it anyway. "No skin off my nose," I say. "If you can take it, I can."

"Right," he says. "You're no wimp."

"Neither are you, O'Neill," I tell him.

"Yeah," he says, and then when he's halfway out the door: "I know."

It's practically pitch-dark by now, but looking out the window I see Dad's left a string of brown leaves running through the middle of the back-yard. If he sees that in the morning, he'll be mad at himself for not finishing what he started. So I go outside, get the rake out of the garage, and drag the leaves down to the end of the garden. I guess that's the kind of guy I am. I guess.

Gretchen

I'd just gotten out of the shower this morning when my mother came rushing into my bathroom, all excited, as usual. "Gretchen, Tina Atwood just canceled on me. I've got no one to hold a sign in Precinct 4 this afternoon."

I pulled one of my big towels off the rack and wrapped myself up. "Mother! Could you at least knock?"

"Sorry," she said, but you could tell she hardly even knew she was saying it, or for what reason. When she's all worked up like that, she can only think about one thing, and everybody else better care about that one thing as much as she does. I remember my dad telling her that before he moved out a few years ago. "You're a force to be reckoned with, Mimi—I'm just tired of doing so much reckoning."

"Get Quincy to drive you to the polling place

after school," she continued. "You'll take over from Carol Modena from three to five."

"I thought you said I could do poll watching this afternoon in Precinct 1." Poll watching is a lot easier. You get to sit down inside a building for one thing, and all you do is keep track of who's voted and who hasn't. Then at dinnertime Mom gets the statistics and calls up any of our supporters who haven't voted yet and guilt-trips them into getting their rears down there before the polls close at eight o'clock.

"I can get an older person to do that. Somebody who'd have trouble standing outside for two hours."

"I don't even know where Precinct 4 *is*," I said.

"They vote at the Eberhardt School. You know, over on Bailey Street."

"No! Oh, Mom, come on, I can't stand over there all afternoon. Everybody in that neighborhood is against us!"

"That's not true. We have supporters there."

"Maybe two people. Really, I don't want to!"

But she wasn't debating the issue with me; I was being ordered. "Take an hour for dinner and then I'd like you to be at Precinct 1 for the evening hours."

"Holding a sign?"

"You present a good front for us, Gretchen. I'm sure nobody will heckle you." She turned around to go, then remembered another command. "Oh, and wear a nice dress, honey. It reflects better on us."

"Are you kidding?" I chased her into the hallway. "It's November! I can't stand outside for four hours in a dress!"

She gave me one of her looks of barely contained disgust. "Well, you *could*. It wouldn't kill you. But if you *won't*, then wear dressy pants, silk or something. Now, don't keep talking to me—I've got much too much to do this morning."

That was how the day began. And it didn't improve much when Quincy came to pick me up for school. I'll admit I was grumpy, which started everything off wrong.

"How come O'Neill always rides with Christine now?" I said (instead of hello).

Quincy's smile faded. "I don't know. I guess they're friends."

"That's weird. As soon as he says he's gay, he gets a girlfriend."

"Whadda you care? All you think about now is O'Neill."

"Don't be ridiculous," I said, then stared out the window glumly for most of the ride before I remembered why I was so grouchy. "Could you give me a ride to the Eberhardt School this afternoon? I have to be there by three o'clock."

He looked at me as if I'd asked him for a kidney. "I have practice after school. You know that."

"You usually drop me off at home."

"Yeah, your house is on the way to the field, but Eberhardt School is way across town. Coach has a fit if we're late."

"Well, we wouldn't want *that*. Just drop me off at home then, and I'll get my own car."

"Yes, Your Majesty. Anything you say."

I wasn't sure if Quincy had been in a bad mood to begin with too, or if mine had just infected him. "That's not how I meant it."

"I know you think playing football is a less noble activity than the way you spend your time, protecting the rights of the wealthy homeowner . . ."

It seemed like I couldn't please anybody anymore, and I just couldn't stand it. "Pull over! I mean it! Pull over! I'll walk the rest of the way!" Which he did and which I did. Not too meaningful a gesture, however, since we were only half a block from school.

• • •

Precinct 4. I got there faster than I intended to because, of course, Quincy was waiting to drive me home the minute school got out. He even offered to drive me all the way to the Eberhardt

School after all, his way of making up. This is
why I fell for him in the first place—I knew we
didn't have much in common, but he was the
sweetest guy I'd ever met. And, of course, the
fact that he's a hunk didn't hurt either.

We were a little more cordial to each other in
the car, but I didn't let him drive me to the Eberhardt School. Partly it was a pride thing, and
partly I'd been thinking I ought to have my car
there anyway, so I could make a quick getaway.
Chances are my mother would forget all about
me in the adrenaline rush of voting day.

Carol Modena was thrilled I was early. She'd
taken my mother's fashion advice and was standing on the curb in her best blue suit, rubbing one
high-heeled foot up and down the other leg, trying to get some circulation going before switching
feet. She'd given up on holding the sign and was
just leaning on it to keep her balance.

"Oh, thank God you showed up, Gretchen.
It was sunny when I got here, but now I'm a
Popsicle." She shoved the sign at me: IT'S NOT
JUST A NAME—IT'S AN IDENTITY! VOTE FOLLY
BAY! Mom's slogan, of course. I'd been work-
ing for the Folly Bay Committee for so long
that sometimes I forgot that it was about
something more than just winning this vote.
Mom made it seem so important—*our iden-
tity*—but at the moment I wondered if it

really made that much difference one way or the other.

"Weren't you smart to wear long pants and a coat!" Mrs. Modena said.

Of course, I didn't say, *Weren't you stupid not to!* I just smiled, presenting my good front. She disappeared into her long black car before it occurred to me to thank her for noticing my good sense. Nobody else had recently.

There was a skinny woman I didn't know holding the other sign, the one that said: IF YOU'RE PROUD OF YOUR TOWN VOTE SCRUB HARBOR! Which seemed beside the point. I mean, I'm proud of my town—I just think it could have a better name. I hated how the whole thing had gotten twisted into who'd lived here the longest and who was more loyal. The town was more than just its name, wasn't it?

The skinny woman didn't even look at me. I figured it would be a quiet two hours anyway, which was fine with me, but just then a car pulled up and I was not pleased to see its occupants. Christine Muser was driving with O'Neill riding shotgun, which was fine. But then the back door opened and who should crawl out but Georgie Pinkus—the most vocal opponent of the Folly Bay Committee at the high school.

O'Neill saw me first. "Hey, Gretchen, are you lost? This is Precinct 4."

"Don't worry," I said. "I brought a compass so I could find my way home."

He laughed at my little joke. I have to admit, the last few weeks since he's come out, O'Neill is so much more relaxed. In a funny way he's more normal *now* than he was before, whatever normal is. I was just saying hi to Christine—who's a little odd, but basically okay—when suddenly there was Georgie Pinkus, glaring at me.

"*You're* holding the other sign?" she said. "Great."

What was I supposed to say to that? "Somebody has to." I smiled, hoping I could kill the witch with kindness, since I didn't have a bucket of water handy.

As Georgie was negotiating the sign takeover with the skinny woman, this tall guy with very black hair got out of the backseat. He looked vaguely familiar, but I couldn't place him. He nodded silently, a little shy, I thought.

"Have you met Ricardo?" O'Neill asked me. "He's from Brazil. He's staying with the Musers."

"Oh, sure. You're the exchange student," I said. I remembered I'd seen him at the park with Christine and Georgie on Halloween. "You're in my science class."

"Yes, I am," he said, smiling.

"No fraternizing with the enemy," Georgie told him. I don't think he even knew what she was talking about. Christine and O'Neill laughed as if she was joking, but it was pretty clear she wasn't. I couldn't believe the poor guy had gotten himself mixed up with Georgie. I could just imagine what he'd tell his Brazilian friends about American girls when he got home: too bossy and no sense of humor.

Christine and O'Neill drove away, honking like they were in a parade. The skinny woman left next, and pretty soon it was just me, the witch, and the exchange student looking at a long, cold two hours.

"Many people are voting?" Ricardo asked.

He had a cute way of talking. "I've only been here a few minutes," I said. "Seems to be a pretty steady stream."

"Which is good for us," Georgie said, grinning. "This is *our* territory."

"We have our supporters here too," I said, repeating the party line I'd argued against only hours before.

"Right," Georgie said, rolling her eyes.

"You are one who like name Folly Bay?" Ricardo asked me.

I nodded. "My mother and I helped organize the Folly Bay Committee. We hope that by changing the name of the town we can help it to realize all of its potential." I could hardly believe I'd said that; it was one of my mother's favorite phrases, which I'd always thought sounded kind of stupid. And now I could almost hear her voice coming out of my mouth.

Georgie made a noise of disgust in the back of her throat, then glanced up at Ricardo. She probably didn't want to look too obnoxious in front of her new beau. You could almost see her facial muscles trying to arrange themselves into a less crabby-looking design.

"Gretchen," she said in an I-am-reasonable voice, "listen to what you're saying. It sounds like what Mr. Flanders says about the USISS kids, how 'we here at Scrub Harbor High are helping them realize all their potential.' It's condescending. They're coming all the way up here every day and doing all the work and then *we're* going to take credit for it?"

I wished I could just become invisible. I couldn't bear the idea of debating these things for two hours, especially if I had to speak in my mother's voice the whole time. "One has no relation to the other," was all I said.

"Of course it does. You rich people think you're doing something so great, you're even helping us poor folks over on the side of town that hasn't reached its *potential*. You're going to show us the way, do us a big favor, even if we don't realize it." She laughed. "Maybe that's what the USISS program should do. Just change all the kids' names: Leon could become Allen, Cor-

nell could be changed to Dave, and Shaquanda
could be called . . . Susie! That would be a lot
cheaper than busing them all the way up here!"

"Look, Georgie, I'm not in the mood to argue
with you right now—"

Ricardo interrupted. "We hope very much
that the town will still go by name of Scrub Harbor. Georgie promise me, if name stay same, she
doesn't move to California." He looked down at
his little pal who was pulling the hood of her
sweatshirt up over her head. "I be *desolate* if
Georgie move way."

Georgie stopped fiddling with the string of
her hood and looked up at Ricardo. "Really?" she
said. All the usual belligerence seemed to drain
out of her face, and she studied Ricardo with a
soft, almost scared, look. For a minute nobody
said anything and I was embarrassed to be looking at the two of them, but I couldn't make
myself look away. Nobody had ever said anything
like that to me, not even Quincy. Georgie swal-
lowed and then said, "You've learned a lot of
English the last few weeks."

He picked up her sign and moved it a few
yards down the block so they could teach each
other a few more new words, I guess, without me
watching. Thank God.

I turned the other way and started greeting
people the way Mom had told me to, saying,

"Hello" and "How are you today?" and "Lucky it didn't rain." Anything to make contact was the idea. I felt like such an idiot—I'd never even seen most of these people before, and I knew I wasn't holding a sign they had much sympathy with. Most people smiled back anyway, which I really appreciated, but the ones who didn't, the ones who turned away or gave me an angry stare, made me feel terrible, like I was a kid with a lot of damn nerve.

The only thing worse was watching the yellow school bus roll past on its way out of town and catching sight of Shaquanda Nichols peering out the window at my sign, laughing.

• • •

By the time my two hours at the Eberhardt School were over I was tired and had a headache. I'd intended to stop at Esther's Cafe or DiCenza's restaurant for a quick dinner—a little reward—before going over to the Precinct 1 polls at the West End Fire Station. Instead I went home, fed Pattypan, took a couple of ibuprofen, and lay on the couch for forty-five minutes, then ate a yogurt and a few saltines driving over.

At least in Precinct 1 more people were likely to be in favor of the name change, so I figured they'd be friendly. What I'd conveniently forgotten was that my mother would be at Precinct 1,

running around trying to prove how indispens-
able she was, her cell phone permanently attached
to her ear. She was scurrying back and forth
between our poll watcher inside the building and
the volunteer drivers waiting at the curb next to
us sign holders. Anybody could call up to get a
ride to the polls, of course, but Mom was more
concerned about making sure all her supporters
got there.

She was giving directions to Nelson Coleridge
when I got there. Was there ever a civic duty Nelson hadn't volunteered for? He waved at me, but
I guess he knew better than to interrupt Mimi
Carstenson to say hello. After he drove off to pick
up his customer, Mom sailed on over to me. I'd
just taken the sign from Mrs. Blackmon, who was
hotfooting it to her vehicle, probably so *she* didn't
have to have another discussion with the Boss.

"*There* you are. I was wondering what happened to you," Mom said.

I looked at my watch. "I'm three minutes late!"

"When other people are depending on you,
Gretchen, three minutes is a long time."

I decided to let it go. There was no way to win
an argument with her anyway; I'd learned that
years ago. "So, how are we doing?" I asked her.

She scowled. "I'm not happy. The voting
numbers are lower for Precincts 1 and 2 than for
any other part of town. I don't understand it."

"I thought you said there were people in all the precincts—"

"A *few* people, of course, but our base of support is here, *our* side of town. You know that." She stamped her foot.

Funny, how when *I* said that twelve hours earlier, I was wrong. Like I said, you cannot win an argument with this woman. "Well, there are still two hours left," I said. "Are you calling people—"

"Gretchen, please don't tell me how to do my job! I've been on the phone for an hour already. Some people are backing out on us—people who all along said they wanted the name change— now they aren't so sure."

"Really? Like who?"

"Like the Pattersons, Mrs. Coldwell, the Sayerses! Your precious boyfriend's family. I would have expected some loyalty from them!"

"I'm not surprised about the Sayerses," I said. "They weren't that thrilled with the idea from the beginning."

Her mouth dropped open and she puffed out a little disgusted air. "If you *knew* that, whose job was it to change their minds?"

"What? You expected me to talk Quincy's parents into voting for Folly Bay? They're adults. I was just working with the kids."

"Kids don't vote, Gretchen. Kids don't *vote*!"

Which meant what? That all the work I'd

been doing at the high school for the last six weeks was a waste of time? Mom's phone rang then, and since she'd had enough of me anyway (and vice versa), she stalked off.

Who wouldn't change their mind after spending so many weeks listening to my mother rant? She could be so annoying, anybody would side against her. I wouldn't be surprised if half the Folly Bay Committee had decided to vote for Scrub Harbor after all, even if they didn't have the nerve to tell Mimi Carstenson.

Nelson pulled up to the curb and got out, then ran around the car to open the door for his passengers, Mr. and Mrs. Evans. They were kind of feeble and Nelson helped Mr. Evans get Mrs. Evans up onto the sidewalk. They waved him away then and he called after them to be sure and let him know when they wanted a ride home.

"Got a lot of business tonight?" I called over to him.

"Not as much as your mom thinks I should." He came over to stand with me. "I guess the Evanses are Folly Bay supporters, but a lot of the older people I've picked up seem to be voting the other way. They say things in the car about not liking change. The good old days. You know." He shrugged.

"Oh, well," I said. "We tried."

"You're giving up awfully easily." Nelson was surprised. "I thought you'd be the last one out here fighting—dragging people out of their warm living rooms at ten minutes of eight."

"I thought so too. I guess I'm just tired."

A car drove up about then and parked right in front of us. "How's it going?" a male voice called out into the darkness.

Nelson and I both leaned down to look into the car. Adam Russell was in the driver's seat, and next to him, her eyes already glued to Nelson: Nadia Kazirenko. I was happier to see Adam than I wanted anyone to know. I didn't really want to know it myself. Ever since that day I'd talked to him on the beach, I'd been thinking about him and wondering what he thought of me, if I seemed different to him than to the kids who'd known me forever. But here he was with Nadia—I guess she turned out to be the one who looked different to him than to the rest of us.

"We were just going out for a pizza," Adam said. "Nadia wanted to stop by to see how the election was going."

More likely Nadia wanted to stop by to see Nelson. Good luck to Adam if he hoped to break *that* spell.

"Not bad," I said, hugging myself. I'd gotten

shivery all of a sudden. "Could be better, but at least it's almost over."

"Ah," Adam said. "Is this what happens to a zealot when she gets cold? Damn the election—find me a fireplace!"

"Hey, you don't want to get her mad," Nelson warned Adam. "She's her mother's daughter, you know."

Which people say all the time. Which I hate. At least Adam didn't know my mother, but I was about to contradict Nelson anyway, to protest that I wasn't really that much like my mother, when Nadia piped up.

"Nelson, are you going to the game on Friday?" It was a bold move for Nadia. I was pretty sure she wouldn't have had the nerve to ask him if she hadn't been in the car with Adam, on what certainly appeared to be a *date*.

Nelson wasn't expecting it. "Well, gee, I'm not sure. I need to check with Shaquanda. We were going to get together and do calculus sometime this weekend."

Shaquanda? More civic duty, or did Nelson have a personal interest? You think you know people, but then they surprise you.

"On *Friday*?" Nadia sounded brokenhearted. "Everybody goes to the game."

"The program kids usually don't," Nelson said.

Did he not get that Nadia was nuts about him, or was he just used to ignoring it? She looked crushed. Adam, I noticed, didn't look too pleased either. *Forget about him,* I told myself. *He pines for another.*

"I'm going to the game," Adam said. "You can come with me."

Nadia smiled kind of sadly. "Sure. I guess."

"Good," he said. "I know Gretchen will be there. Can't miss her boyfriend's big game."

"Nope," I said. "Can't miss that." I'm such a great girlfriend.

Just then Mom started yelling for Nelson. The Evanses were ready to be driven home. He said a quick good-bye and ran to his own car. I thought Nadia would break her neck trying to keep her eyes on him. Don't be dumb, I wanted to tell her. Here's this cool guy who likes you—cooler than Nelson, who just isn't interested no matter how much you want him to be. Wake up and smell the pizza!

After they left I didn't talk to anybody else, just stood there doing my monotonous job (*Hi! How've you been? Nice night for November!*) until about seven forty-five when Mom finally came marching over.

"You might as well go home," she said. "It's over. The town has let us down."

"We lost? You know already?"

"Haven't you been listening to me? Yes, we lost. I can tell by the numbers who voted in each precinct." She heaved a weary sigh. "I guess the committee just didn't work hard enough. Next year we'll start sooner, we'll go to Town Meetings, we'll—"

"Next year? You're going to do this again?"

"It's something I believe in, Gretchen. I thought you did too!"

"I did, but if the town doesn't want it, it seems like a waste of time—"

"We have to convince them they *do* want it. That's where we failed."

After so much work and such a lousy day, I really didn't feel like talking about where "we" had failed. Besides, convincing people they wanted something that they really didn't came a little too close to Georgie's analysis of the committee's intent.

Mom brushed her fingers against my wrist, which for her is heavy-duty physical contact. "Of course you're focused on your immediate future, as you should be. Our next project is to get going on your college applications."

"I can do them by myself. I don't need help."

"Gretchen, I've read up on this. At least I'll help you with the Wellesley application—"

"I'm not going to Wellesley," I said. I didn't even know I'd been thinking about it, but when she said that, it was clear to me one decision had already been made.

She stopped for just a second, then rolled on. "Don't be silly—of course you'll get into Wellesley. With your grades and my legacy—"

"I mean, I'm not applying. I don't want to go to Wellesley, Mother. That was your school. I want to find my own place."

"Gretchen! You don't know what you're talking about. Wellesley is the perfect school for you. I loved it there!" She was looking at me as if I had a gun pointed at her head. This was definitely a betrayal.

"I know you did, but I want my own place to love."

"Where would you go that's better for you? Tell me! Where?"

"I don't know. Maybe someplace in California or Oregon. Someplace different."

"Since when have you wanted to be different?" There was the hint of a smile on her face. She thought she had me now, that I *liked* being a cookie cutter.

"Since today," I said.

She waved her hand in the air, dismissing such a silly thing. "Oh, well, this is a rash idea. Stemming from exhaustion, no doubt. We're all exhausted. Get a good night's rest and then we'll attack the next project together."

I handed her the sign and walked to my car. She thought she'd won, that I was giving in to her again. But there were other ways to win a dispute. Maybe I looked like Mimi Carstenson on the outside, but on the inside I was Gretchen, whoever that might turn out to be.

•   •   •

By ten o'clock my mother had rallied what was left of the Folly Bay Committee and they were drinking coffee in our kitchen, making lists and charts and diagrams for next year's battle. I was in my room, wrapped in my bathrobe, looking through the stacks of catalogs that had arrived in the mail the past few weeks when I was too busy to care. The ones that looked most interesting were from Stanford, Pomona, and Reed. Places my mother had never even seen.

When the phone rang I knew who it would be.

"Hey," Quincy said. "You doing okay?"

"I'm fine," I said. "Thawing out."

"I heard the returns are going against Folly Bay."

"Yeah. Scrub Harbor didn't want a new identity."

"I'm sorry."

"Why? Nobody in your family wanted the name changed anyway."

"I know. I'm just sorry because you *did* want it."

"You know, I'm kind of glad now we didn't win," I said.

"I must have the wrong number," he said.

"No, it's just that I'm already starting to feel like I don't live here anymore. So whether the town changes its name or puts up a high-rise office building on the beach, it doesn't really affect me. If the Folly Bay Committee had won I would have felt responsible for making a lot of people really unhappy. This is *their* home, not mine." I wasn't sure Quincy knew what I was talking about—I wasn't too sure myself.

"You might come back after college, though." He didn't make it a question, but I knew it was.

"I don't think so. I'm not the type to live down the street from my mother." Although if you'd asked me last week I might have said I was.

Quincy was quiet for a minute. "How *is* your mother?"

"Oh, she's great. She loves to fight. Now she'll get another year of it."

"And how about you? Do you like to fight too?"

"No, I don't, Q. Let's not do it anymore."

"I'm for that." He sounded relieved and I realized this was the real reason he'd called. He was afraid we were breaking up and he didn't want to. Not yet anyway.

"Quincy, I want to change when I go away to

school. I don't want to be Mimi Carstenson's identical twin. I want to be somebody different, somebody my Scrub Harbor friends wouldn't even recognize."

He gave a soft laugh. "I'll always recognize you."

"You will?" I wasn't sure whether to be flattered or annoyed.

"Sure. At our twenty-fifth reunion I'll be able to pick you out from across the room."

I didn't say anything. I couldn't begin to imagine who we'd be in twenty-five years.

After a minute, Quincy continued, "I'll say to my wife, 'See that woman over there, the pretty one who looks so confident? She used to be my girlfriend.' And my wife will be jealous because, after all those years, I haven't forgotten you."

You think you know someone, but then they surprise you.